The Birth Control King of the Upper Volta

The Birth Control King
of the Upper Volta

Leon Rooke

ECW PRESS

CANADIAN CATALOGUING IN PUBLICATION DATA

Rooke, Leon
   The birth control king of the Upper Volta

ISBN 0-920802-48-6

I. Title

PS8585.064B57   C813'.54   C82-094904-3
PR9199.3.R65B57

The publication of this book has been aided by grants from the Canada Council and the Ontario Arts Council.

Five of the stories in this work have been previously published in *Antaeus, event/journal of the contemporary arts, Canadian Fiction Magazine*, and *The Fiddlehead*. An earlier version of 'Sing Me No Love Songs, I'll Say You No Prayers' appeared in *Epoch*. All others are published here for the first time.

Typeset by Howarth and Smith Limited (Toronto) and printed by The Porcupine's Quill, Inc. (Erin).

Published by ECW PRESS, Stong College, York University, Downsview, Ontario.

Contents

For Earl and Evelyn, and for Donald

The Birth Control King of the Upper Volta

THE MOST EXTRAORDINARY THING happened to me today. I woke up and discovered I had lost yesterday. Amazing! Not a slither, parcel, or dot of it remained. Yes! The sun was dazzling bright, my entire room was lit up like a store-front. I stretched, I yawned, I kicked off my sheets: oh lovely, perfect lovely! — is what I said.

Absolutely. That's how innocent I was.

And here I am forty-seven years old. You'd think I would have had a hint.

Dogs outside my window were having a romp. Squealing, yowling — how I had slept through their hubbub was more than I could imagine. Yet I felt wonderfully excited. Renewed, you might say. 'What a dreamy day!' That's exactly what I said to myself — and right away set about performing my exercises. A somersault. Another one. Nothing broke, thank goodness. My room is so small I have to do these flip-flops on a pin-head. But the exhilaration! — I truly felt superb, even while lifting my barbells. Twenty, thirty, this is too easy, I told myself — add more weight! Add a ton. I slid on the ton. Ten, twenty, thirty — no trouble at all. I could have gone on all day pressing these feathers, with barely a pause for breath.

'Oh you're fit,' I said laughing, addressing my form in the mirror. 'You're in peak condition, Adlai!' I pulled on my pants, scooped back my hair. Washed my face and neck in the little sink, eager to run down to breakfast. 'Eat a horse,

Adlai,' I said, 'yes you could. What an appetite you've worked up! Hurry up, now!'

Ah, what a babe. What an innocent. For it was then, hustling through the door, that I made the discovery. The beautiful calendar hanging by the nail drew my eye. And why not, for pictured there was my sweetheart, Greta Gustafsson. I always notice her, entering or leaving. Sultry woman, she'd mope — she'd scratch out my eyes — if I didn't. Everyone needs noticing is what Greta would say. 'What a beauty you are,' I said, rubbing my cheek against this image. Kissing her bare shoulders. Greta moaned. I moaned also. 'Good morning, my darling,' I said. 'Sleep well, my beauty?' She lowered her eyes. This morning she seemed preoccupied — seemed distant. My heart ached. Greta deserved better than I could give her. She deserved, in the least, a silver frame, a wall with a good view. Yet as it is there is hardly room for myself. For my footlocker and narrow bed. The walls! — stretch out your arms and there you have it. And so ugly! Uneven and fly-specked — filthy! — with immense zigzags cracking all about.

'No, the door,' I said, smoothing down her hair, 'the door is best for you, beautiful Greta. Don't complain. Don't scold. Things will be looking up for us once I get that job with the Pole. Give me a smile, darling. What would you like for breakfast, my honey? Say the word and I shall get it.' I kissed her eyes. Greta likes that. She purred. Oh Greta adores eye-kissing. My perfect Greta.

But wait, for here's the news. Drawing back, I happened to glance at the date. Mercy! 'What's this?' I asked myself. Impossible. But yes, there it was. Yesterday had disappeared. Had become, I mean, today. What *do* I mean? I mean at that very second I discovered there had been no August ten in my life. The bold red type was clearly announcing itself: August eleven — anniversary of Blondin's crossing of Niagara Falls on a tightrope wire, so the little historical note informed me. *'God help me!'* I cried, *'I've lost yesterday! What happened to the tenth?'* Greta giggled. Then she saw my stricken face and fell quiet.

8

Gone, I thought. One whole day! Jesus God!

I stumbled out into the hall. Voices floated up from the dining-room, jibber-jabber, everyone talking at once, the way they always do. Slurp-slurp — you'd think I slept above a hog pen. Jibber-jabber, slurp-slurp — what imps!

'I say,' I called, 'what's the date down there?'

Silence. Not a word. You'd think I had dropped a giant brickbat on their heads. And out of the stillness came Mergentoire's sprightly reply: 'Wednesday! It's Wednesday, you ape!'

Ape? Ape? What had got into sweet Mergentoire?

'Idiot!' I screeched. 'Get control of yourself, woman. The *date*, what's the *date*?'

More silence. Utter stealth, you'd have thought. One would have sworn the entire table had fallen asleep. Then Mergentoire's voice again, laughing this time, shrill as a rat: 'The eleventh, you rogue! Wednesday the eleventh. The day Blondin went over Niagara on a tightrope!'

Then the clatter of dishes once more, and everyone else shouting up the hideous message too. Chomping away on pancakes, scraping back in their chairs — where's the butter, who's got the milk jug, *oops!* — that sort of thing. All the confusion and turmoil, the belching and bellyaching you get when twenty hard-hat labourers are trying to gulp down their protein before rushing off to their jobs. No shilly-shallying, I mean, quick-quick, sorry old mate, got to run!

What a waste of man and woman's best hour. My old mam and I, we would sit for hours about the breakfast table, munching carrot sticks, dipping our bread into tea, perusing the journals and up-to-date magazines, rattling the tabloids.

— 'Ah, son, here's another one.'

— 'Another one, my mam?'

— 'Guinea-Bissau, this one's called. How many does that make, son?'

— 'I don't know, my mam. What's your guess?'

— 'I count forty-one, son. Forty-one since your old Daddy went into the field.'

9

— 'That's a lot of emerging nations, my mam! That's a whole hodgepodge full! Oh, they are really carving it up. What do you think old Daddy would say, my mam?'

— 'He'd say "roll me over, dear. Roll me over in my grave and throw another white right on top of me." '

— 'Tell me about it, my mam.'

— 'It was the Upper Volta that broke your old Dad's heart. Oh, son, when they let the Upper Volta go they as much as put a dagger through his chest.'

— 'Cold-blooded murder, my mam?'

— 'That's right, son. It was a mean, depraved act and who's to reap the whirlwind now?'

— 'Us, my mam?'

— 'That's the bite of it, son. But eat your carrots, Adlai, they don't grow on trees and a boy needs to hoard up his strength.'

I went back into my room, thinking about poor old mam and all the black African hordes yet to sweep down. Crossing the water on rafts and matchstick canoes, beaming their great white teeth and kicking their great black legs, all to gobble up our jobs and steal our women and make a garbage hole of our neighbourhoods. 'Not yet, my mam,' I wanted to tell her. 'Adlai is holding on. Old Adlai's got the biceps and the brawn, he's got the will-power: you won't find him kissing no woolly hair.'

I could see old mam nodding her approval even as I stared with remorse and disbelief at my calendar's lost date. Where was yesterday? Old mam would say the blacks had got it, just as they'd take away anything else I'd be foolish enough to leave lying about.

— 'That's right, son, they got it. They'll take the shoes off your feet if you don't tie them up tight!'

Greta Gustafsson gave me her alluring smile. I swayed in close, putting the kiss of sin into her smouldering eyes.

'I *vunt to be alone*,' she whispered, turning away.

My heart skipped; it always puts me in a torture, seeing Greta in her moods.

'But Greta!' I whined.

'*Yoo lust a day*,' she murmured, resentful and hurt. *'They are my days too and I hold yoo responsible.'*

I dropped down on my narrow bed. Scrunching up my toes, for there was not enough room for my feet between it and the wall. Something fishy going on here is what I thought. Adlai, you've got to use your wits if you intend to figure this one out.

Days, I thought — as you would have yourself — just don't disappear.

I consulted my diary, lying open on the footlocker table. Lying open to August ten. To the day that had never been.

7:00 — wake up, lazy-bones! Exercise. Wash. 7:30 — Pancakes with the gang, mmmmm! 8-6:00 P.M. —job, uggg (but don't complain!). 7:00 P.M. — Talk To The Pole. 8:00 — Home. Dust room. Wipe sink. Exercise. Bedtime snack. Shut-eye. (And no messing about with Greta.)

'Oh there's monkey-business afoot here, Adlai,' I said — for it looked to me as if I'd a very busy day. And why not? — a thousand irons in the fire, things to get done, people to see! Life to *live*! My old mam, looking at my diary, would have patted my head. She would have said, 'That's dreamy, son. That's top marks. How you get it all done is beyond me. Oh yes, you're a chop off the old block.'

So.

So I'd say myself.

Yet I was blotto. I had not even the fumes, not even the ashes, of my past day. Zero.

Greta was sulking, giving me first one cold shoulder and then the next. Drop dead, is what Greta was saying. What a disappointment you are. What a rathead. 'You expect too much of me, Greta,' I told her. 'I do the best I can.' But she flounced her hair and thrust out her chin and drew the cloak of gloom over herself.

A *hard* woman. A *tough* woman. Just, I thought, like old mam.

So I forgave her. I decided she was right to be mad. I had

let her down. I had promised her she would be safe with me. That I had what it took to keep a good woman happy.

A newshawker was shouting his headlines out on the street, and I rushed to the window. 'You!' I yelled, 'what's the date?'

His startled black face sought to find mine.

'August 11, boss,' he said.

The dogs were still fighting in the dirt, squealing and yowling and spinning in a fury.

'Are those mongrels yours, boy?' I asked.

'Not mine, boss.'

The dogs momentarily ceased their yowling to blink up at me. Then they went back to it with renewed ferocity.

'Well then,' I asked the boy, 'what's the news today?' And he held up his grim headlines to me:

SUMMIT TALKS COLLAPSE

+

AUTO-MAKERS LAY OFF ANOTHER 30,000

+

INFLATION HITS NEW HIGH

My world, I thought, and still there.

'That all, boss?' asked the black face.

And when I didn't answer immediately, he did a little soft-shoe.

It seemed to me I'd seen him before — him or his twin — standing in the line-up to receive his dole, wearing butter-yellow shoes, a red eye patch, a watch-chain long as his arm — and streaming off in his big Rolls-Royce with three bois-terous women white as white eggs and laughing like mud-flaps.

But was this true or was it my old Daddy sending his vision across the licking water?

'Listen, kid,' I called, 'did I buy a paper off you yesterday?'

His black face grinned up at me over his watermelon. 'Not off me, boss. I'm fresh brand-new in the country, first day on the job.' He danced a swift jig along the pavement, playing a mean tune with his harmonica comb. 'I aims to make my fortune, boss,' he chirped. 'Me and my fourteen brothers looking no way but up. We got a toe-hold on progress. Gonna git our relatives in. From here on out de sky is de limit!'

I slammed my window down on this strapping young grinner, and proceeded to do one hundred push-ups — a few headstands — to work the vitriol out of my system. It had been the vitriol that had slammed down my old Daddy and made his gums bleed. That had turned him boots up.

— 'What killed him, my mam?'

— 'Vitriol, son. When the blacks painted up their bodies and screamed their heebie-jeebies he was filled up with vitriol and flung himself into the first river.'

— 'What was he doing there, my mam, in the distant Upper Volta?'

— 'Selling birth control to the Roman Catholics, son. No easy job.'

Greta was breathing hard. Clenching her fists as she strode this way and that. Hissing. Stopping me cold with her hot fury. I knew what was on her mind. She wanted me stepping up in the world. Wanted me out of my red suspenders and into top hats. She wanted me to call up the Pole, find out about that job. I stole a look at her, wondering. Trying to figure out what it is about women. Why they drive their men so hard. Why they can't be satisfied. It crossed my mind that I wasn't cut out for a go-getter like Greta. That I'd be better off with some redhead lounging back in a bikini on a leopard-skin rug, selling fertilizer to farmers. With someone all bosom and legs who would say, 'I'm for my man, right or

13

wrong. My man is a macho-doctor, good for what ails me.' But I didn't think this long. Greta was my heart's need, my solace, my joy. Without her I'd be swinging on vines.

So I stepped out into the hall to make my call.

Mergentoire, I noticed, had put up a new sign: DON'T HOG THE PHONE. This was tacked up beside another one that said NO CALLS AFTER 8 P.M. And another one, dripping blood, that said THIS MEANS YOU.

'The Pole here,' the Pole's voice shrieked in my ear. 'Speak up!'

But there was thunder overhead. Then the thunder was rumbling down from the third floor, down the stairs, driving towards me. 'Out of my way, fat man!' came the nasty cry. Wong, the slant-eye. I shrunk back, hugging the wall. His yellow face whirled past, bumping me — hurling himself off to his job. Late again. This Chinaman, one more of the numberless hordes. 'Fat men!' he screeched. 'Always fat men! Never looking where they're going! Always hogging the phone!' He clattered on down, flinging back more abuse.

A big country like that, you'd think they'd stay in their rice fields.

The Pole was shouting, too. 'Who is it? Speak up! I haven't got all day!'

I gave him my name.

'Oh,' he said. 'Oh, it's you! The nincompoop! What's on your mind, nincompoop? Why are you bothering me?'

Hold on here, I said to myself. Why is the Pole addressing me in this unseemly fashion? What gives? It had been my impression that the Pole, more than most, held me in high regard. Respected my talents. Why otherwise would he have been trying to give me a job?

'If it's about that job,' he now was saying, 'you can blow it out of your stove-pipe. I told you yesterday. I've hired someone else. I got some foreign bird at half the pay. Strong! Eight feet tall! Can't speak a word of English. But I'll work the stink off him, don't worry about that!'

And before I could get my wits raked clean the rascal had hung up.

Poles, I thought: what can you say about Poles?

I thought: what a relief! Changing jobs, what a nuisance that would have been! I mopped my brow, thinking: what a close call!

Anyway, I told myself, I like the job I've got. I'm happy. Greta's happy, what's the worry?

I slouched back into my room, feeling pretty good.

'It's the Pole's bad luck,' I told Greta. 'He missed a good bet. Hiring me was his golden opportunity.'

Greta wasn't talking to me. She had put on one of her hats, the one with feathers. Plumed like a cavalier. Scooped low, the brim shading one eye. String of pearls at her throat, as if she intended going some place.

Well, I didn't mind. I liked to see Greta all dressed up.

But she had fire in her eyes — a torrid spitball.

'*Rats!*' she hissed — or something like that.

Her shoulders arched back as she paced, pivoting her hips. I watched those hips, those eyes, stole glances at her flat chest. She looked so luscious, so mysterious — so magnificent and sure of herself.

I wanted to hug and hold her, to weep in her thighs.

But I put the brave face on. 'That Pole,' I said, 'he must have been out of his mind to think I wanted his soft job. Me, at a desk! What a laugh. None of that white-collar malarkey for me. I like being outside breathing in the fresh air. Hauling those rocks. Working in rain, wind, snow. Working up a good sweat in the hard freeze. A man's work, that's what I'm cut out for.'

Greta's cruel veil of derision fluttered down.

— 'It keeps a body fit, my mam. In tune with nature. It's nice being out there where only the fittest survive. It's educational, old mam. Not a day goes by I don't tip my hat to old Darwin the theorizer.'

I could swear my old mam had walked right into the room. She stood not a foot away, shaking a finger.

— 'So long as you don't get the heebie-jeebies, son. That's what done in your Daddy. That and the vitriol.'

— 'I've heard it said he was a drinker too, my mam.'

— 'Envy, son. The envy and malice of small minds. It was the envy of him that spread that story.'

— 'And womanizing, my mam? Was he a womanizer, as I've heard?'

She sat down on my bed, spreading her hands palms-up on her lap. She had a spot of soot on her chin, and watery eyes. I reached over and brushed away the soot. Her hair had a singed odour, as if she'd fallen head-first into a smoker's flame.

— 'Womanizing won't kill a person, son. There are some as would say it's what keeps a body going. But your Daddy wasn't like that. And if he had been, it isn't likely he would ever have touched black. Now listen to me, Adlai. You listen good. Three thousand nautical miles separated your Daddy in the Upper Volta from us where we were, not to mention umpteen years — but your Daddy's eyes were always looking back home. He kept his heart and his eyes dead set on us. On me and you. He put love first, but he knew he had that. Had our love and our trust. But he was a committed man. An obsessed man. I've told you a thousand times: your Daddy had a mission to protect us, and others like us. Our very way of life. And he went with my blessings. I remember the very day he left I said to him, "Go and do it, Humpter, and do it well, and always know you have me here thumping my feet for every success you have." Humpter, that was my secret pet-name for him. Everytime I would call him Humpter he would blush. Yes, and I would too, for we were just newly-weds, you see. We still had the rice in our hair. But I knew my duty. And he knew his. So he pecked his mouth to my cheek and said to me, "You're the one woman every man dreams of! You know a man's duty comes first!" — and then he shook my shoulder, and left. It was so beautiful, so beautiful the way he said it that I broke down and cried.'

— 'Did I cry too, my mam?' I asked. But old mam was gazing off into the blue, as if she were back there with him, and didn't answer me straight-out.

— 'What's that, son? What did you say?'

She had a clump of mud down on her knee, and I brushed this off. Her old skin was leathery and brown and there seemed to be mites running in her hair. This, or some trickery in the air.

She was giving my walls and the room the hard-eye.

— 'Is this the best you can do, son? Why this room is hardly bigger than a burying hole. And look there! You've tracked dirt all over the floor. Don't you ever clean up?'

— 'Down on my knees, mam, every evening. Down with soap and rag, just like you.'

For old mam always had; she'd liked a place clean.

— 'Not *last* evening, son.'

— 'No, old mam. Something must have come up.'

— 'Excuses won't get you into paradise, Adlai. I'm only glad your Daddy isn't here to see it. And that!' she said, pointing — 'Who is that? That smoky-looking temptress up on your door?'

I made way to introduce my sweetheart Greta, but old mam was having none of it. *'Shame, baby, shame!'* she was saying. She stretched back groaning on the bed, letting her feet flop over the edge. She still wore the same ankle-high work books that had mesmerized me in my childhood. They had the rot of thirty years messing about with turnips and spuds, a lifetime of kicking at grass and dandelion. The laces were covered with mold. The socks on her thin bones were both shoved down.

Old mam closed her eyes.

— 'Are you going to take a nap, my mam?'

Greta was hissing at me to get that woman — 'that *voh-mahn*' — out of here.

— 'I never shut my eyes in the daytime,' mam sadly replied. 'No, nor sleep in the night-time either, if you want to know the truth.'

— 'Why not, my mam?'

She reached up — as though dreaming — and with a small sob stroked bent fingers across my cheek.

17

— 'From worrying about you, son, the way I never had to worry about your Daddy, though I'm pained to say it.'

— 'Why's that, my mam?'

I crouched down, my face only inches from her bird-tracked skin. I was pained, too, and jumping with nerves. My mam looked a thousand years old, all helpless and withery and done-in. I wanted to fling myself down across her bosom, and moan. To say, *Old mam, what's happened to us?* For I had lost a day and my life was going nowhere — but where had hers gone? She smelled musty and — well, *moldy*, — as if she'd been put away in some high cupboard and left there a long time, and now had come down all wizened and crusty.

But I stayed still. I couldn't bring myself to hurt or confuse or embarrass old mam.

— 'There are moments, son, when I think you don't care about your old mam. Moments when I wonder if you don't think I brought you up wrong. Times when I think you are holding me responsible for so much that goes on in this mean world.'

— 'I'd never think that,' I said, half-horrified.

— 'Or that you don't revere your Daddy, that you don't uphold his cause.'

— 'No, mam!' I cried, 'how could you think that?'

She was gripping my hand tightly, her mouth twitching. Her eyes boring up into mine. Yet she looked so ancient, so feeble, so ahead of or behind her times. Her brow as wrinkled as a scrub-board. The flesh so speckled. It was as though a flock of perky chickens had got loose to scratch at her skin, which sagged down over her bones — but all so thin it was practically translucent.

— 'Oh don't look at my face!' she suddenly cried out. 'Don't stare at me like that! I know what you're thinking! Know how you've turned against me! How you've come to hate your own flesh and blood!'

This speech utterly amazed me.

— '*Me?*' I said. '*Me*, my mam!'

For I'd always thought of us as close. As tight, I'd thought, as nectar and honey.

Mam sobbed. She rolled over, burying her head in the pillow. I eased down on my footlocker, shivering for her. Slowly stroking my hand up and down her backside. Saying, There, there, mam. There, there, good lady.

A fine little weave of bones was about all I could feel.

Her body felt cold. Cold and *icy*. And moist, too. And there arose again that smell, all earthy and wormy, as if she'd washed up from some foul pit or tomb, some ill and dank un-resting place.

— 'Don't worry,' I soothed her. 'Don't trouble yourself, old mam. It was us together through thick and thin for all of those years. For *so many* years. And I tell you the truth, I never knew one from the other, never knew thick *from* thin, that was how much I knew I could count on your love. True, old mam. And it's how much you can count on mine now.'

— 'Do you mean it, Adlai?'

— 'I do, mam. I sure-as-shooting do.'

She clawed at my hand. Grappled my fingers up to her lips, and kissed them. 'My man,' she sobbed. 'My little man. My comfort in this sick old age.'

We had us a good cry.

And I think old mam might have dozed, for I saw her breath slacken, felt her bones soften and smooth out underneath my stroking hand. I might have dozed or day-dreamed myself — dappled off on beams of sunlight — for at any rate when I next blinked my eyes back to it the aura in the room seemed to have changed. It seemed as if not just minutes but hours, days, whole weeks, had tumbled by.

The dogs were setting up a din outside my window, snarling and yowling.

I could hear Mergentoire at the foot of the stairs, shouting up at me. Get off the pot! Quit slacking! Get a move on! Saying she wasn't holding breakfast all day. Not for the likes of me. Then growling at her son Hedgepolt. Telling him too to shake a leg.

Women. You'd think they were shot from the womb to ferret out wrongdoers and hobnail them to a pristine trail.

What a nag.

Greta was in a huff, down on her knees on the floor, going at the dry mud-tracks with a scrunched-up hat. At *my* mud-tracks, or so it appeared. For they had my hoof-print. But who? How come? Greta throwing up insults at me: *ape* this and *ape* that. She is such a puzzle, Greta is. Aloof much of the time, yet now ready to scratch out my eyes because I had let my own sweet mam walk in and take a moment's rest on my unmade bed.

Isn't Greta funny? I thought. Oh how I wish I knew what makes Greta tick!

But my stomach was growling; I needed my pancakes fast.

— 'Mam? You feeling okay?'

Mam sat up, wiping her wet cheeks with the backside of one frail hand.

— 'Oh,' she said with a brave smile, 'it was just like in the old days, us having that good cry. It has done my heart good.'

— 'Mine too, my mam.'

She patted my head — 'That's a good lamb!' — then hopped up spiry as a cat with four legs to catch herself and knowing she would. 'Time's a battlefield, son,' she gaily observed, 'but thems that's got the backbone will whack through it to the other side.'

— 'I'm whacking, mam,' I said. 'I'm whacking hard.'

Her eyes lit up; the old colour came back to her cheeks. 'Yes, you got the backbone, the same as your Daddy did. I only hope you got his grit. That you're willing to stand up for what's-what.'

— 'I will, mam. You can count on me.'

She came in for a big hug, and I could swear she lifted me right off the floor.

— 'Don't get me wrong, son, what I was saying earlier. I'm not renouncing any of the ways you were raised. I don't apologize for swat. Right is right, and a mother has got to stick to that. No, it was just your Daddy's ghost preying on my mind. Me feeling low, wishing I could be with him. They broke the mold, you know, when they made him.'

— 'He stood tall, that he did.'

She stared off, all misty-eyed. Her hands up to her temples, looking back to those days. 'Poor man, it was the birth control that sapped him. Think of the pressure he lived under. Imagine the Upper Volta as it was the day he set foot there. Two hundred thousand Roman Catholics reproducing all over the place. They're like dogs, where two drop down ten more will pop up. So that was the RC's. And that's not to mention three million Mossis with the soles of their feet white as yours or mine and every bit as busy. Or half a million Lobis, another half-million Bobis, plus the thousands of itchy Gurunsis. Not one ever having heard of birth control until he came. And everyone black, black, black! The brightest sunshine makes no difference to a continent like that. Daytime or night-time, you'd never know it. That's what so many blacks can do to a country. Your Daddy had to walk about with a good Eveready just to tell one black hole from another, and hope he didn't fall in. A woman wanting a baby she'd fall down in a ditch and let the men poke at her. That's all there was to it, so your Daddy said. It makes you sick, don't it? Just thinking about it. It does me. But your Daddy was no cry-baby. He was not the man to tuck tail under his britches and run. No, he kept plugging. Kept singing the glories of birth control. He knew it was *us*, our very way of life, our very freedoms, that he was defending. He knew all about their matchstick canoes; knew they'd soon be finding their way across the water. That they'd take our jobs, gut our neighbourhoods, throw down and have their mean pleasure with our women!'

She stood trembling, radiant with his memory, yet sickened by the reality of that other vision.

— 'I know it, my mam. I take my hat off to him the same as I take it off to you.'

— 'So I thumped my foot and said "Go to it, Humpter. It's your job and you do it well." '

— 'He did it too, mam. He sure did.'

Mam vacantly nodded, still trapped back there in time with him. I saw her little foot tapping; saw the worship flare in her eyes.

— 'You were tops too, mam,' I said. 'You kept the home fires burning.'

Mam smiled, in a drowsy, far-off way. Her voice went all wispy:

— 'Now and then I'd get a sweet letter from him. "Chalk up another one," he'd say — and I'd know he'd saved another white child his rightful spot in the world. Another white boy his freedom. His job, his sweetheart, his neighbourhood. And I'd go down on my knees, saying: "Bless him, bless him, bless Humpter, for that spot he's saved could be my Adlai's!" '

— 'He did it too, my mam! He saved my spot! Except for him I bet this very minute some black man would be standing right here where I'm standing. That bed would be his, and the footlocker would be his, my barbells, and probably he'd even have Greta!'

But old mam had switched off. She was beginning to have that tuckered-out look again. She seemed to be fading.

— 'It was always my hope,' she said wanly, 'that one day you'd take up your Daddy's mighty cudgel.'

My head sagged down. I looked dumbly at my shoes.

— 'I did, Adlai.'

I had been dreading this remark since first she entered. I looked miserably at my dirty thumb-nails. Whimpering:

— 'I'm sorry, my mam.'

Mam stared right through me. Her tongue slashed like a lizard's:

— 'As it is, you haven't even married. You don't even have children.'

I saw Greta suck in her breath. Saw her face go scarlet.

— 'Nary a one,' continued mam. 'No, you've let your spot, and your children's spots, go to some gang of unruly, howling blacks! You've let the blacks take charge!'

Old mam, I knew, did not mean to hurt. She was only expressing her disappointment in me. Telling me how my Daddy would hang his head.

— 'But remember I'm whacking, mam! I'm whacking away. I've got Greta! I've got that Pole I was telling you about!'

But Mam wasn't listening. She was simply smiling her sad understanding at me. Smiling her sad, abandoned hope; letting me see how her dreams and my Daddy's dreams had got splattered by the whirlwind. She laughed, trying to lighten both our loads. 'Thick and thin,' she said, 'it doesn't rain but it pours.'

— 'I'll shape up,' I moaned. 'I'll shape up yet!'

Mam was slowly buttoning up her coat. Her fingers were gnarled and spotted. The colour of oatmeal. Nothing but bones. Somehow the soot had got back on her nose. Her hair was like wires. Even as I looked, her finger-nails seemed to be growing. Her cheeks were sunken. She had on her favourite coat. The coat was faded and tatty and hung unevenly at her heels. I remembered that coat. She'd got it off some hook at the Bingo Parlour. She had the little gold locket around her neck. Heart-shaped. My Daddy's image would be on one side; I would be on the other. If, unbeknownst to us, some black face hadn't jumped in.

She backed, groaning, out into the hall. Her finger beckoned to me. 'Our kind is no more than a spit in the bucket,' she said. 'You remember that. It's all one big tub out there and what part isn't filled with blacks is stacked up to the brim with Chinese. It's over-flowing with Poles and A-rabs and Indians and even Huguenots. That's another bunch your Daddy didn't like, them Huguenots. And the whirlwind's coming. But that don't mean we toss in the towel, does it, son?'

— 'You bet!' I said. 'You bet, my wonderful old mam!'

She was already vanishing. Holding up her old Victory fist.

— 'One more thing, son. Get that tarty woman off your door.'

Folding back into the wall, becoming the wall. Stumbling once or twice and then . . . gone. Yes, gone.

Yet I hung in the doorway, hoping for one final glimpse.

— 'Mam?' I whispered. 'Mam, are you still there?'

I ran over and kissed the wall. Put my cheek where her visage had been.

— 'Mam?' I said. 'Will I see you again?'

But she *was* gone. Wall or world, it had swallowed her up. And I stood trembling, pining for a sweet farewell. Longing for one unsullied word of love. Wanting total forgiveness — full recognition — from her.

Afraid — shivering with fear! — that my Daddy next would walk in.

Sighing. Unable to admit that what I wanted most was what I never could have. This: that *both* would leave me alone.

And Christ, which way *now* could I turn? For I wasn't out of these woods yet. I made out Mergentoire at the foot of the stairs, stomping the floor, shaking a spoon.

'I've told you!' she shouted. 'Told you and told you! Breakfast this minute or you go hungry!' And spun off.

Hedgepolt, hidden away, was banging on pots and pans.

The dogs were nipping and yowling.

Inside my room Greta was heaping up rage. Barking out her scorn. Quite furious.

'*Kooom* here!' she ordered.

Defiant, sullen, raving Greta. My angry beloved. She'd come down out of her calendar to wipe up mud and listen to the prattle of old mam. To stride the cramped room, to whirl contemptuously about and with guttural, raking voice — dramatic as a blizzard — declare that she had never been so insulted, so humiliated. So violated and abused. '*Like dirt I am treated! Yes? No?'* To ask what kind of flea or toad was I, what creature, what snivelling worm, what formless, horrible, gamboling idiot? *Yes? No?* To ask how *'dot voh-mahn'* could dare invade our privacy, rumple our sheets, question the way we conducted our lives. *'Who is dot death-hag to tell me I shood marry, I shood haf children! How dare she? Und did yoo see dot coat? Dose shoes? It's lunacy, sheer lunacy, und I, Greta Gustafsson, I moost put with theece!'* To rail at the callousness, the bigotry, the inanity, the perversity — at the dim-witted nature of mankind in its totality and my blood-line in its particulars.

'Vy do I stay with yoo?' she shouted. 'Vy do I make myself preet-tee? Vy did I ev-vair koom to theece half mahn, to theece child, theece mental deficient! Vot a place your room izz! Vot a stinkhole! I haf seen shoeboxes big-gair. Me, Greta, who has lived in palaces, who kood haf kings with the krook of my fing-gair!'

'Oh!' she cried, galloping about, thumping her fists against my head, wrenching up and down. 'O-O-O-Oh! De an-sair is only one. *Une!* Me, I am craze-eee too! Greta is birdbrain!'

This Stockholm beauty, what a flame-thrower! What acid! And how beautiful. How divine. How my heart soared to see her in this mood. Sultry. Passionate. Maddeningly dramatic. I had seen her a hundred times this way on the shimmering screen: breathing this fierce energy, this mystery, this power. A dynamo of unrelenting love. Yielding only *to* love, no matter how fatal. Love came first, above her very life. Her every performance insisting that love *was* life. That every risk was worth the taking. *Mata Hari. Camille. Ninotchka. Wild Orchids. The Blue Sea. The Yellow Bed. Anna Karenina.* — Garbo. My very own Garbo. The great Greta Lovisa Gustafsson. Yet never so in my little room. Always the cold shoulder, the blank stare, the senseless smouldering — elusive, self-absorbed, afraid of her shadow! *Above* life.

'Liar!' she now screeched. *'Yoo haf not loved me enough! I haf not vunted your idolization! I haf vunted to be loved as I am! As you haf loved your lunatic old mam! Greta does not*

vunt to be alone! She does not vunt alvays to be on de vall. Hold me, darling!'

Oh Greta, Greta, Greta. This much I now knew of Greta, as I was coming to know it of myself: every encounter, including those only imagined, is an affair of the soul. Is cut-throat war. The soul is at vigil; it is in last-ditch battle. It is in armed conflict against the grinning dark, the waiting terror, the foul abyss. It holds off the stinking Hereafter. The soul would defend and preserve our tenuous and fleeting bones. This pitiful, slime-sinking body. Soul is heroic! It goes on warring despite impossible odds of stone and brick-bat and the immense conflagration, the high flames that ever sweep around it.

This I find remarkable.

Nothing else in life is so beautiful.

And Greta now accepted this, too. Greta was willing. *'Any-zing!'* she now wept. *'I vill do any-zing to hold your love! Even theece ugliest of rooms, theece flea-box, theece hole, theece dot! Let it be ours! Hold me, Adlai. Hold and kiss and save your demented Greta!'*

Oh, what a speech! My flesh tingled. Bells clanged in a thousand towers. For we were saving ourselves. We were dis-covering again that one body alone cannot hold back, cannot assuage, bend, or diffuse the wicked dark. The vile, thunder-ous, rampaging dark. One's frame falls apart, bones scatter, flesh flies apart like birds over water, but true love, true life, charges on. The bones explode, they mix with air and water, with air and flower, and when they come down they come down rearranged. Love, dreadful love, slouches in.

And so her lips plunged down on mine. The famous Garbo mouth burned, burned and parted. Our tongues slithered and slid like a hundred snakes uncoiling in a single wet hole. A wet, luscious, heavenly bog. We moaned — exultant! What a picnic! What a dreamy, wondrous, spine-tingling dark! What ecstasy! For mouth was nice, but mouth wasn't all. We locked limbs, we licked and scratched, we yowled

26

and bit and spun. Howl, spit, and claw. What a whimpering, roaring, blood-boiling feast love is! The floor scraped at our elbows. Knees cooked. But our singing flesh went on multiplying. Steel replaced backbone. Fire replaced lips. Hands tugged and stroked, tongues slurped, our hips hummed. *Hmmmmmmmmmm!* Our hearts clanged like a Cyclops' thunderbolts. We crashed against the footlocker, kicked against wall, and came grappling — breathless! — up over it. We slithered as one onto the crumbling bed. The mattress sizzled. Smoke shot from my ears. The roof lifted right out of my skull. And still our tongues went on working. For mouth was nice but mouth wasn't all. Matters got deadly. The hum quickened. EEEEEEEEEEEE!!!

'I want you, Garbo!' I thundered.

'Dun't talk, idiot!'

We romped past passion, past love's fury, and settled in for holy worship of piquant — exquisite — lust. And I thought, as I have always thought: What a treasure woman is! What a world! What a dream-time! Oh, wow, Adlai, how lucky you are!

The first time.

The first time ever.

My baptism.

Soul's immersion.

Thus when it was over I still couldn't believe it. Impossible. Greta had wanted *me*? Pitiful me? I studied her sleeping body, amazed. Her little feet! What extraordinary toes! — like the curved white petals of flower. Her bent knees and the fingers so softly folded. How fragile she seemed. The chin tucked so childishly into her bosom. Her breath so faint, so sweet, so . . . *not there* . . . that I wanted to convey it into heaven on a quivering rainbow.

This dream had wanted me? Uncanny. No, it was beyond truth. Reality couldn't touch this.

But I touched her — one finger along the ribs — and knew that it had.

27

'*All the news you want!*' shouted the black vender. '*Get it here, boss!*'

I went at last down to breakfast.

Mergentoire and her son Hedgepolt sat at the massive table, alone but for each other and a sea of soiled dishes. The steaming atmosphere of daily exhaustion and a mother's eternal, despairing vigilance. What wreckage! Oh the appetite, the furnace-stoking, gut-storming wizardry of twenty hard-hat labourers at their meal! Reaching, sweating, chomping — packing in the fuel. My brusque, unroped companions from the mines, the factories, from field, ditch, and stable; our century's dogly warriors. Our last heroes.

Mergentoire was slumped low, brooding in half-doze, raking a hand idly up and down Hedgepolt's spine. The boy didn't hear me enter; he stayed limp as a rag. Mergentoire's eyes shifted grievously to me. 'Here he is,' she moaned. 'The man who doesn't know what day it is. Who doesn't know today from tomorrow or yesterday from a mile of cotton candy.' She looked away dreamily, scratching away at some itch under her bra strap. 'How was the funeral?' she asked softly.

My eyebrows went up.

I sat down.

Mergentoire's mood underwent another subtle shifting. She glowered, hoisting a heavy arm in the direction of my room: 'I could shoot you,' she said, 'for what you do up there.'

I grinned sheepishly into my lap. My body was still humming: the hum was silent, but I yet had it. *Ummmmmmmm.* Like ripples on a lake when the sky is becalmed.

Mergentoire sighed heavily. 'Well,' she said, 'if there's anything left, feel free to gobble it up.'

The bread dish was empty. The fruit dish was too. No eggs, no porridge. The coffee pot had six drops left in it.

I didn't mind. My stomach was motor-boating away but my head was off in dreamland. My thighs still had the quiver.

Mergentoire's voice softened again. 'The old lady,' she said, 'I hope she went happy. I hope she'd made her peace with God.'

I was studying Hedgepolt, who had a fly trapped in his hand. He opened his fingers slowly, but the fly remained as found. In his palm's centre, faintly buzzing, mindlessly grooming its ugly head.

Mergentoire and I stared at the fly. We stared at Hedgepolt as well, though it was the fly we kept returning to.

Hedgepolt poked a finger at the fly. The fly flipped over and lay on its back, unmoving.

'The old lady,' murmured Mergentoire. 'How did it go?'

But I hardly heard her. What about that? I was thinking: Hedgepolt has a pet fly.

'The funeral, you ape!' growled Mergentoire. 'How did it go?'

The fly lifted, banking away.

'Did anyone come? Did she have flowers?'

Whoa, I thought. *Whoa*, Mergentoire. What gives here? For I knew not at all what she was talking about.

Yet, as I blinked at her my confusion, something tapped at my eyelids. A dim, grey shadow lifted on the previous day. The littered table gave way to rain-soaked ground.

Leaning headstones.

A black, snarling sky.

Rain thundering down.

My shoes sloshing through muck.

Wind whistling past my ears like shrieks from a shut-up thing.

Hedgepolt's sticky hand in mine.

Mergentoire saw something too. And looked to see if she could find evidence of it in my trembling hand. In my besotted eyes.

Whoa, I thought. Whoa, Mergentoire. Let's not go too fast.

— 'I was up all night cleaning his shoes,' she said. 'Lucky for you he didn't catch cold.' She eyed me shrewdly, raking a

29

coil of hair back behind one ear. Tugging her housecoat up to her throat. 'Well, I'm not the one to say it, and God forgive me, but what I say is you can count your blessings she's gone.'

Whoa, Mergentoire.

'I mean, she was *old*. I mean, she's out of her misery now.'

Hedgepolt, I noticed, was now studying me. His mouth opened a little wider. His eyes too. Drool coagulated around his chin.

'Hello, Hedgepolt,' I said.

He closed up his hand. The fly had returned.

I can't understand Hedgepolt and here's why: he looks to be every bit of thirty, yet he's still in grammar school. Still wears his trousers rolled to his knees, still has a runny nose. Can usually be found sucking on a filthy dishrag. I call it so; Mergentoire calls it his security cloth.

This morning he didn't have the cloth. His great head was slung out over the table like an ironing board. Studying me, when he should have been training his fly.

'Say good morning, Hedgepolt,' Mergentoire told him.

Hedgepolt blinked. His tongue slipped out. Slowly he dipped his head and began licking at a clear spot on the table.

I laughed, though his behaviour made me uneasy. This was regressive conditioning, it was backsliding. It went against the pact I had with him. Even so, I went on laughing. 'Hey, Hedgepolt,' I said, 'who's your mam?'

His eyes jiggled, he straightened rigidly in his seat — then his arm flopped up to point directly at me.

'Good old Hedgepolt,' I warmly murmured. Touched, as I always was, by this odd familial display. Such a good-hearted, agreeable lad, I thought. I leaned over and roughed his hair.

Mergentoire glared.

I ignored her crossness. We all have such days.

'It won't work,' she snapped. 'It's time you faced up to things. The old lady —'

But I cut her off. 'The boy needs a haircut,' I said. 'He needs to give more attention to his appearance. One of these days old Hedgepolt is going to start thinking of girls.'

Mergentoire's face went red. She caught her breath. Her fists bunched up and her close little eyes stared angrily into mine. 'Not under my roof he won't,' she said heatedly. 'Not while I live and breathe!'

Hedgepolt was nodding excitedly, a grand smile on his face.

We had had talks, him and me. I'd set him straight on the birds and the bees.

'Look at him,' I said. 'He's ready right now. You do want a girl-friend, don't you, Hedgepolt?'

He was nodding as Mergentoire's fist slammed down. She was genuinely fed up now. 'Stop saying that!' she cried. 'Stop dreaming dreams for my Hedgepolt! Quit giving him expectations!'

I thought: *Ah, that Mergentoire, what a case!* I thought: *Dream the dreams, Hedgepolt. Dare to be God!*

And Mergentoire's face drained. She rose up, clutching a fork, clutching the folds of her loose gown — fit to be tied. You'd think she had stepped right into my head: 'So it's God now, is it?' she raged. 'It's God you want him to be? When he can't even go to the bathroom by himself!'

I thought: *Small stuff, Mergentoire.* Thought: *Poor Mergentoire.*

For Mergentoire disliked the interest I took in her boy. Hated the care I had taken in grooming this boy for a normal life. It alarmed her, our walks in the moonlight, our talking of birds and bees. The way he hung onto my every word. Nor could she admit to herself the long way he'd come, under my wing. *A sea of expectations*, I thought. *A sea for everyone.*

'God!' she shouted. 'When he can't even tie his shoes? When he doesn't even know what shoes are for?'

Hedgepolt was crying. His wide thick shoulders shook and actual tears were splashing down. One quivering hand reached for the table-cloth. He tried stuffing that into his mouth. Terrible. Oh, what sounds. I knew he was suffering. I knew the hurt he felt. I ached with him. But a mere six months before this he'd been docile as a turnip patch. Empty. A vacuum. His face had never revealed the faintest expression, beyond a stony watching. He had never cried.

It hurt. But this was progress.

Mergentoire whimpered, embracing him, tugging his head to her bosom. 'Don't cry,' she whispered, sobbing herself. 'Oh, don't cry. Mam's sorry. Mam got out on the wrong side of the bed this morning. Mam's sorry she raised her voice. Forgive your Mam? Forgive me, Hedgepolt? Mam would never hurt her Hedgepolt. Mam loves Hedgepolt.'

Beautiful. I loved Mergentoire at her mothering.

'Let's see your fly again. Let Mam and Adlai see your nice fly.'

They went on blubbering. And, yes, I did too. For I was remembering my own old mam. I was back there with her, my head on her bosom. Sobbing. Getting charlie horses in my gut from all the ache I was carrying.

— 'There, there,' she'd say. 'You're thinking of him, aren't you, son? Of the good Daddy you've never seen? But don't cry. Don't blubber. You know your Daddy has got his work to do. Just as one day you'll have yours.'

— 'Will I, mam?'

— 'Sure you will. Your spot is saved. It's waiting for you.'

— 'Mam? My mam? Did he ever try it out on you?'

— 'Try what, my boy?'

— 'His birth control.'

— 'Oh gracious. Goodness gracious. Of course he did. I was the first.'

— 'But mam!'

— 'It didn't take, son. Otherwise, would I have had you?'

— 'I'm here, am I not, my mam? I'm *real*?'

— 'Oh you're real, son.'

— 'Are you sorry, my mam? That I'm here?'

— 'Now, son, don't cry! Don't blubber. Hold those shoulders back. Don't you want your Daddy to be proud of you?'

— 'Will he be? Will I grow up to fill his fine shoes?'

— 'Oh I doubt that. There can be only one of him. And there's this to think about: long before you've come of age the black tide will have swept over all of us.'

— 'But my *spot*, my mam!'

— 'I've upset you, haven't I? There, there. Mam's sorry. Give a kiss to your potty, unthinking old mam. Mam got up on the wrong side of the bed today. That's it — give a smile to your old mam.'

Dear wonderful mam. Dear comforting mam. She was aged then herself, and her back stiff from weeding spuds. From keeping together house and home. Between my Daddy and the bingo I was all she lived for.

— 'Is that true, mam? Am I your pudding and pie?'

— 'You're it, Adlai. The apple of my eye.'

— 'I wasn't dropped off on your doorstep? By some man on a black horse?'

Mam would get cross when I'd ask that. She'd get out what she said was my Daddy's old walking stick, and switch my behind.

— 'Who's been telling you them stories? Putting these tales in your head.'

For it was a fact I'd been hearing things. There was talk that mam wasn't all she said she was. That mam had never wed, for one, and that'd I'd come down the chimney like a chimney-black.

— 'Lies! Lies! Don't listen to them!'

But I'd been wondering. Not all I'd heard was going out of both ears.

— 'They hint that I'm tar-brushed, old mam. That there's a tar-brush somewhere! That there's not smoke without fire!'

— 'Hush! Hush! Don't even whisper it, child. Your Daddy is away yonder in the Upper Volta doing his work. You're making his ears burn.'

But I'd find myself looking and wondering. For something else was occurring. Putting the heebie-jeebies on me. I'd look at mam's elbows and her knees. I'd look at her hands and feet. I'd examine her skin. I'd catch her with her housecoat undone and I'd think: *that's* strange. For it seemed to me mam's skin was changing. That her flesh was darkening with every day that went by.

— 'What's happening, my mam?' I'd say. 'What's happening to you?'

And mam would cover up her face, she'd shiver and shake.

— 'It's old age!' she'd moan. 'It's my . . . my Change! It . . . it's from thinking all the dark thoughts of a lifetime! It's . . . from having you!'

And I'd laugh. Old mam, what a joker.

But later I'd be looking in mirrors. In bed at night I'd be feeling my hair. A bit *stiff*, I'd think. A bit *wiry*. A bit on the black side.

And next day I'd nag at old mam. I'd say, Mam, don't you have a photo of my Daddy? Don't you have *one* picture of him?

Mam would thump her chest. 'In here,' she'd say. 'In my heart, that's where your Daddy's photo is. And in yours, too, if you had any decency left.'

Sweet, dear old mam. Her stick was hard on the behind, but she was ever straight with me.

The dogs' yowling, and not Hedgepolt's weeping, broke up my reverie. They'd come yowling three times around the house and twice up the nettle tree, and now had parked under the dining-room window to kick up dust and yowl all the harder. It was blood-curdling murder out there, with maybe a cat or two mixed in.

I nibbled on a toast scrap from the neighbouring plate. I licked on bacon rind found under the chair.

It didn't matter. Appetite was the last thing I had.

I was remembering a letter I'd received. *Dear Son. My spot's about used up. I'm slipping. Not long left now. Will you come? Can you do that for me?*

I hadn't gone. No, I'd let her dot fade right out.

34

August 11: anniversary of Blondin's crossing Niagara on a tightrope wire. And mam stretched out in a box on the rain-soaked ground.

'Do you love me, Hedgepolt?' Mergentoire was asking. 'Do you love Mergentoire most in the world?' She had his head on her shoulder, was stroking his hair. Her voice soothing, even to me. 'Your mam loves *you*,' she said. 'Adlai loves you too. We are all one big family.' Her foot nudged mine under the table. 'Tell him, Adlai. Tell him how happy we are.'

For Hedgepolt's sake I managed a smile. A nice little nod of the head. 'You bet,' I said. 'She's said a mouthful, son.'

Hedgepolt's robe-chewing slackened. His eyes widened. His look swam from her to me. 'Brace up, Hedgepolt,' I said. 'Life has its little monkey-wrenches, but you can follow my example.'

And I sat erect, my shoulders back, my expression firm. Pretending I was looking intelligence at him. Happiness, too.

We sat a long time that way.

Strangely, his face shook loose of its idiocy until at last it became one radiant angel's smile.

'*Dad-dee,*' he said.

Our jaws dropped. Hedgepolt had never been known to speak before.

'*Dad-dee,*' he said again. And his arm flopped towards me. Then with more grace than I could believe he swung it around to point at Mergentoire. '*Mam-mee!*' He patted her head.

Mergentoire's lips quivered. Her eyes glazed over, then moistened. With a deep moan, half-sob, half-joy, she swooped her arms around him. But Hedgepolt's own arm kept on rising. His face was flushed, his heart pounding; I could see he was getting the hang on speech. '*Gret-ta,*' he said. '*Gret-ta Gus-*TAFS*-son!*' He wheeled about, beaming. Dashing to the window. '*Dogs!*' he cried. '*Brutish, snarling dogs!*'

Mergentoire bolted up. We were both dazed. For a

moment we shared an uncomprehending look. Then bliss streamed out of her pores. *'You're cured!'* shouted Mergentoire. *'Oh, Adlai, he's cured! My son is cured!'* She embraced him, lifted him off his feet, swirled him around. *'My baby! My baby's no baby no more!'* And she — and both of them — broke off into riotous laughter. They danced and hugged and jumped on the floor. But Hedgepolt was still wanting to talk. He was stammering in excitement, wanting to get it all out:

'Shoes!' he crowed. *'Adlai and Hedgepolt get shoes wet? Walk in muck? See old Mother? Throw flower in grave? Kiss old Mother goodby? Walk home in rain? Adlai hold Hedgepolt's hand? . . .'*

He spoke on, radiant. And joy, pure joy, in that moment seemed to serenade my bones. It seemed to seep up through my chair and to surge through me like light through a door. And it went on blazing. It went on rising. It shot up through the long table, rattling the dishes; it pulsed over our heads, and spun; it crashed up into the ceiling and went on rising; it crashed through our very walls and went on splashing and tumbling, whirling like a fireball through the atmosphere. Even the dogs, vicious that second before, fell silent. Joy rolled on, flooding the universe. And even then it swept on, shining and beautiful.

We were all in rapture.

'Adlai happy!' screeched Hedgepolt. *'Adlai happy for his old mother? He happy for Hedgepolt? He happy with world?'*

Hold on, I thought. Adlai, hold on.

For it wasn't mam I saw, or Hedgepolt's glee, or the two of us reeling over mam's sorrowful grave, or mud on our shoes. These were but a flick at the eyelids. Joy, purest joy, was shunting these aside. What I was seeing was deep water and over the mammoth face of that water legion upon legion of matchstick canoes and in those canoes a thousand black faces and those faces whooping delight at me the same as I was whooping it back at them. And nothing poor mam could do about it. One by one they were crying out, *I'm coming, I'm coming, make way for me! I'm going no place but* UP UP UP! Oh look at the Devil running! Flags I saw waving by the hundreds. There were the Upper Volta colours and beside it little Benin and Guinea-Bissau. Over there were Gabon and Cameroon, Ghana and the Ivory Coast. Here came Somalia and Djibouti and Botswana, Nigeria and Malawi and Kenya. And a great chorus was riding the waves: *We coming! We are coming, brother!*

Hold on, I thought. Hold on.

For I could hear myself shouting back, as if from a planet a breath's space removed: *Come on, you polecats! There are spots for all of us!* The Upper Volta ears picked up. Their eyes did a double-take. *Is that you, boss?* they asked. *Is that you? Is that the king?* And I gave them my biggest wave: *Come on! Come on! Git the lead out!* At this, the Mossis, the Lobis, even the itchy Gurunsis, scooped their hands into the water, rode the crests of waves, and came crashing forward. *We coming, boss!*

Crashing on past me as I sat rocking in my chair — in my chair or wherever my spot was — delirious in the face of this vision, wondering which was vision and which was real life and finally where it, or they, or even myself, had gone.

Something wet was licking my hand.

My scalp felt tingly.

This day, too, I thought, was slipping away from me. The light seemed eerie. Had I slipped forward into some future year? Adlai, where are you? Adlai is on his tightrope out over the swirling water, balanced between rope and sky, wavering and floundering with his balancing pole. Adlai steering for the river's other shore. Adlai saying Mam, are you there? Mam, will you forgive me? Adlai falling. Adlai crying. Then only the quivering rope and the crashing water there.

'You've done it, Adlai! Hooray for you!'

What's this? I thought. What's happening now? For Mergentoire was hugging me. Hedgepolt was hugging me. And I was hugging myself, too. I was trembling inside a rapture

37

totally new and strange. What a mystery! Sweat dripped from my nose. Is this happiness? I asked.

I could hear Greta upstairs gaily chirping. Calling to me. 'Adlai, come draw my bath. Come up and scrub my back and sit with me.'

Mergentoire and Hedgepolt were silent. Their eyes rapt.

The dogs beneath the window were silent. Or gone. I thought I could see them racing as a pack down the long street to another place. Soon, perhaps, to splay off into green countryside.

I closed my eyes.

Peace.

Soul's ascension.

And mam's watchful eye splayed off, too. It went whirling away into the dark.

'Adlai, are you coming?' Greta called.

I had the strangest desire. I wanted to say to Greta: 'Go home, honey. There are people at home who have need of you.'

But I said nothing. I stayed on. Stayed, I say, as if bolted to my chair, as Hedgepolt's head lay warmly in my lap, and Mergentoire leaned against my knees, emptied of her joyful weeping. I sat on, thinking: So many people in the world depend on you. So many. Even if you're nothing — even if you're no one and you don't know which way to turn or whether turning is a thing you're capable of — even then they do.

Oh, mam, they do.

Sing Me No Love Songs I'll Say You No Prayers

BINGO DUNCAN AND THE CLOTHES-LINE

Now Bingo Duncan started out in the logging business first as a choker-setter working the dog chains behind a five-ton Cat and graduated from this to second-loading, which is easier on the lungs and limbs as it is more stationary, but all of this was in his carefree youth, those good wild days before he ever set eyes or anything else on little Judy (one hundred and sixteen sweet pounds and every inch sugar to his tongue, when eventually the wild days came to that). By the time he got to Northern Cal and the Sundown Company job he was a full-fledged sawman who could trolley the big blade with the best of them, and Judy, bless her heart, weighed a good deal more than the one hundred sixteen sweet pounds he had bargained for. But as she liked to say, he was not much of a bargain himself. Only kidding, you know. On arriving in Cal he got a job sawing for Arcadia Lumber at their plant up in the Wichapec range, and kept it until one day the floodwater carried their plant out to sea (and me with it, Bingo was fond of telling, had I not been hanging onto Judy at the time. Them flash floods rooted up Redwoods and hauled bears out of the tree-tops but my Judy never budged a mite. Glad I had been feeding her so good). Month after month after this Bingo haunted the Eureka employment office and watched some drab spit of a man write in whitewash on the window the jobs available thereabouts. Nothing decent, nothing permanent, nothing that might bring solace or sunshine to his pounding, urgent heart.

'Just *toe* work,' Bingo told Judy. 'Bottle-washers and gas pumpers, clerks and manure-stompers, seems that's all the world has need of nowadays. How I wish —'

'Wish, wash this dish!' Judy would say. 'Wish, take this garbage out, and while you're at it bring in my clothes off the clothes-line.'

BINGO AND JUDY AND HOW PRIDE PRECEDES THE FALL

'If you weren't so high-and-mighty, Bingo Duncan, you'd go south and pick the fields. The Wetbacks do it, why can't you?'

'I am your Logger Lover, not no Wetback who roots for two bucks a day.'

'You and monkeys, scratching's all some monkeys know.'

'Rub it in, Judy. Hit a man while he's down.'

'He's down, but is he prone? Then here I come with my spreaded knees.'

BIG JUDY, PAST, PRESENT, AND FUTURE

She was born, she said it herself, to take what a man had to give and to give it back to him in the way nature liked best, in the form of a darling child. One or two to start with, then four or five, five or ten. More's less the worry, or so I've heard. I was made to bear offspring the way a hen's good for laying eggs. And I am plumb fed up with them ramrod women who hate the sight of a friendly child's face, with them who think the sunshine stops after birth of the first. Me, I'd as soon have a whole houseful.

Periodically over the years she stopped strangers in the supermarket aisles, touched their shoulders on the street, saying: 'I swear all that man of mine has to do is look at me and I'm pregnant again. It takes a big, solid woman to stand up to a gift like that.'

BLOWS A MELODY FROM THE PAST, SOME DISCORD IN THE WINGS

Out here, west to the sea, falcon and cormorant riding the

breeze — out here Bingo said a man could breathe. He could fill up his chest, fill up his eyes and ears, and feel something of the sky's sway — something of God's power — in his own mean little mind and soul.

'I swear it,' he'd say. 'I been a different person since I come out here.'

Out here a man could roll back his sleeves and work up an honest sweat. He could rely on his biceps and his brains. Work was easy on the troubled mind, fine medicine for the tumble-down heart.

'Look at Judy,' he'd say. 'She ain't stopped smiling since we came.'

But what now? Where's work now, now that Arcadia got washed out to sea? I'll tell you, there's a cruel wind blowing nobody no good. And what's my Judy gone and done? What has that woman let happen to herself? A year ago I could lift her off the floor with one hand. Now look. It grieves me to see all my wild oats come to this. Lord help me, yes.

For in the meantime she had given birth to the first bleeding youngan and the second was pressing at the gates.

'He's pressing, Bingo. I can hear his little nose going rat-a-tat-tat.'

All as Bingo cursed the employment man for his HELP WANTEDS and the Wichapec range for its floods and the earth for not bowing when a good sawman stood. Meanwhile, Judy took a job at the All-Nite Highway Cafe down on 101. 'What's it matter,' she'd say, 'if a mother-to-be has to plod and plod.'

My pride, Bingo would think, watching her go, ain't what it was.

THE SUNDOWN COMPANY: BRINGING YOU UP TO DATE

I could have told you, Judy told Bingo. I could have told you from the start.

Where's the start? asked Bingo. Where's the end? I been told and told, since the day I first stepped from the womb.

Well, you stopped listening somewhere. You got your ear

to your own hurts and that's all you hear now.

Sundown, a wildcat gypo outfit, was on its last leg the first day it opened for work. Hit and run. That's the kind of seedy outfit it was and what Judy would have told him. Sundown had taken over and whipped into almost working shape a deserted mill far up Wichapec road, 57 miles from the nearest town. And that barely what you would call a town. Bingo heard about the job opening at six o'clock one morning, standing outside the employment office window blowing on his hands, stomping his boots to keep warm. Fit to be tied. Wondering why he bothered.

Pzzzzt.

Yeah?

A driver who hauled timber on his own truck, patron of the All-Nite Highway Cafe, sidled up to him, saying: 'It's a lot of much, ain't it, we ought to gone into politics.'

So?

Bingo didn't like him. He didn't like drivers in general, and especially those who owned their own trucks. It made him sick, just the way they got in and out of their cabs.

Listen, the man said. I had a talk with the little lady.

Who?

Your old woman. Sweetest face I ever saw. When *that* woman blows in your ear I bet you listen. I know *I* would.

Yeah?

Things rough, huh? Having a rough patch? That's what the little woman said.

It's rough all right. Not a pot to piss in and it's been that way since the flood. Manure-stompers, that's all the world has need of nowadays.

I got news, said the driver. You interested in news? You bring your lunch-pail?

I got it right here.

He lifted up his lunch-box and they looked inside. A roast beef sandwich, an apple, and three cookies wrapped in the tinfoil of a Camel package.

Up on the Wichapec, the driver said, this here sawman fell

off his sawman's seat into the belt run. Carried him all the way up to the waste chute to the scrap pit. Nearly fried his ass. They was still working on him when I come down with my load.

There's a job? You saying they need a new man?

They find wine, nothing but wine, in his Thermos jug. One drunk skunk. They give him the boot while I'm standing there.

What is the company?

It ain't much, let me tell you. A gypo outfit they call themselves the Sundown Company. Bunch of scabs. Union wouldn't touch it. But they say they paying ten-twelve bucks the hour for a steady man.

That's it. I'm their man. Hell, I'd work for nothing.

But when Bingo arrived up Wichapec he found the Sundown was only working part-time, hardly enough to keep the machinery from rusting any more than it already had. They could not get enough logs to work full-time, he was told, and the equipment kept breaking down, too — mysteriously.

Mysteriously? How you mean?

We don't know. There ain't nobody can figure it out. It's like the whole damn operation is jinxed.

They did not pay good wages either. The sawman's pay was eight dollars the hour, take it or leave it. Nor had the former sawman simply fallen off his work seat from too much drink. The boss-man and four or five others had given the matter a close look-see. And they didn't like what they had found.

What you mean?

Well, the bolts holding up the seat was right rusty. Could'a been the bolts just gave way. It happens. I mean, the machinery is old and tired. But I don't know. Sort'a looks like somebody might'a taken a hack-saw to them.

Christ!

Anyway, the seat give way and the sawman tumbled down onto the pulley. Poor bastard was lucky, he might'a been sawed up into a two-by-four. But he only broke his leg.

His leg?

That's right. The belt carried him to the scrap pit, then the chains caught him and carried him up the waste chute. Poor bastard was about to drop off into the cone burner. He decided to jump instead.

You don't say.

I ain't saying nothing. Nothing about no hack-saw, anyway. But that's what I hear.

I'll be damned.

You're one of us, then. Glad to have you aboard.

Late that evening Bingo slung a jacket over the baby and drove in his pick-up to the cafe where Judy stood, she'd told him, ten hours a day on her feet, with no rest for the weary. He found her sitting in the corner booth, lapping up a hamburger steak and a big pile of mashed potatoes. First thing she did was reach over and wipe the child's nose.

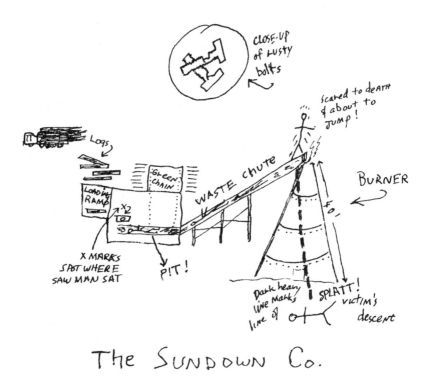

The Sundown Co.

He's awfully runny, she said. I hope he ain't coming down with nothing.

Then she fed him a spoonful of potatoes.

Did you get the job?

Bet your sweet ass, Bingo said. Although take my word for it, it ain't much.

What's it like up there?

So Bingo borrowed her pencil and drew Judy Duncan a map of what had happened and how it looked from a bird's eye.

What's mysterious about rust? said Judy. That child's sleepy. You best take the little honey on home.

Me with it, I guess, said Bingo. I got to git up before the cock crows if I am to hold this job.

BINGO AND HOW HARD TIMES HARDLY GOT BETTER

On good days, with no breakdowns, Sundown might cut 50,000 feet of lumber, which was good enough God knows, Bingo said, but those days together with the bad did not hardly pay enough to pay the rent or the grocery bills for Judy back in the Eureka outskirts where each morning he left her. The days got leaner and leaner, but not Judy still at her job, and each time Bingo dipped the big blade into a log and sliced it along easy as cucumbers he thought with some distaste how it took a lot of money to upkeep a big woman like her, who wouldn't slice at all.

Worse luck yet, he found he missed her.

What my wild oats have come down to, he would say to himself, is nostalgia. What I have got a bad case of is sexual longing.

On one of the leanest days of all he met Crow Kay G.

CROW KAY G.

At the time Bingo met Crow Kay G. both were working the Sundown job but Crow Kay G. didn't have any Judy. He had nobody. All he had was himself and he meant to hold onto that.

45

'So buzz off,' he told Bingo. 'I already met all the people on this earth I ever want to meet.'

THE WORKING DAY AND CROW KAY G.

It took a lot of money and horsepower to upkeep a big woman like Judy but there was one thing saving his hide, Bingo figured, and that was that on the good days no less than the bad the equipment broke down and when this happened it always happened right after they'd started up for the day or when they were about to close down for the night — or in the afternoon just when things were humming — and as the breakdown hardly ever lasted for more than twenty minutes or half an hour the company had no choice but to pay the men simply for standing around. There was a lot of talk about how the equipment managed to break down so conveniently for the men and it was more and more that Bingo Duncan began paying attention to Crow Kay G., a nondescript little bastard with red hair whose personality took on the weirdest change when something in the mill broke down, like some ratty little thing that had come up out of a mud puddle, smiling. He had the wickedest secret smile about his lips, with his eyebrows shrugged down over his nose, and all but about to wet his pants from excitement — so much so that Bingo eventually concluded that maybe Crow Kay G. was going out of his way to bring about these breakdowns.

There was more to this redhead than met the eye.

The little snot was a saboteur.

Maybe. You wouldn't want to say a thing like that out loud. And if he was, then Bingo and every other man on the place was indebted to the squirt for much of their earnings.

COMMUTING

Bingo daily had been driving up and down the twisty curves of the Wichapec in order to be with Judy and the kid and to see when and if the baby would come.

'This here drive is breaking my back,' he told Judy one night. 'I can hardly live on the three or four hours sleep I'm getting.'

'Well, shoot,' said Judy, 'why don't you see if there's a place up there we can live? I've worn out my shoe-leather and need to slow down some myself.'

THE ONE-ROOM SHACK

This morning as usual Bingo got up at four o'clock, with the whole world dark as a witch's bottom, and he drove up the high Wichapec to be there at seven, but this morning he had Judy and the youngan with him and because of that and Judy wanting to brush her teeth and wrap the child up tight and because the pick-up was groaning from so much extra weight, this morning he arrived late. And every man waiting, for what could a mill do with no one in the sawyer's chair? So he hopped right out of the cab and went running.

'But what about me?' cried Judy.

Bingo flung out both arms, shouting: 'The shack! The shack! Go to the shack.'

MORE ON THAT

Earlier in the week Bingo had come to the boss-man with his problems.

'I got me a woman due,' he'd said.

'Do what?' the boss man replied. And when this matter had been cleared up the boss-man had looked Bingo over, skeptically observing that he had not taken him to be a family man.

Why not?

Well, you seemed to me to be just another guy sowing his wild oats, footloose and fancy-free. Now I see better. I see you got those scowl lines down your jaws and the worried eyes of a man looking at a lot of responsibility. Still, I don't see what Sundown can do for you.

I heard something about some cabins.

Cabins? Those old shacks, you mean? Why, they don't have no heat. They don't have no water. No furnishings. All they've got is rats and vermin and God-all. They're not fit to live in.

I heard tell that redhead was living in one.

47

You heard wrong. Where that redhead is living is in a big house off in the woods that some crazy Indians built. Anyway, he don't care where he lives. For all I know he is part Indian himself.

I reckon me and Judy are out of the same boot. We'd like one of them shacks.

Suit yourself. They're free for the taking.

THE UPSHOT OF IT ALL

'What do you think?' Bingo asked Judy some time later.

'That thing! The roof's broke. The windows are all cracked. There ain't no front door. It's *small*! Where will I put my washing machine?'

'It's roomy — for one room. It's got walls. It's got a floor. I could rig up a stove out of one of them big drums out in the woods.'

Bingo asked the youngan what he thought. But the child had broken out in an ugly rash all over his body and could think of nothing but scratching himself.

'I guess it will do until something better comes along,' sighed Judy.

'It's free,' said Bingo. 'It will be different with a woman's touch. Let's see what we can do.'

AN UPLIFTING ENCOUNTER

That day while Judy had been waiting in the truck, feeling mortified on account of how Bingo had left her, the bossman stuck his head in at her window.

'Hear you're about due, mam,' he said pleasantly to her.

Judy's face lit up. 'Yes, it's like all Bingo Duncan has to do is look at me and I'm that way again. I never saw a man with such a natural gift.'

'And what's that there little tow-head's name?'

'That there is Bingo Two. He's my pride and joy.'

'He's a humdinger, that I can see.'

'Say hello to the nice man,' Judy told the child.

But Bingo Two only buried his face in his mama's bosom

and would not come up for air or say hello no matter how hard Judy yanked at him.

'He sure is a humdinger,' said the boss-man. 'Well, best of the day to you, mam.'

And the boss-man trundled back to his chores.

This exchange uplifted Judy considerably.

WHAT BINGO AND JUDY COULD DO

What they could do was not much. Bingo built the stove out of the drum and put in window panes and slapped together a door out of scrap lumber and burned a great heap of rubbish in a cleared space out back. He got the snakes out and most of the rats and he knocked in a new beam to prop up the roof.

Judy put up curtains of a kind and hung a few calendars on the walls and wore out several brooms. She put a flowering bush out in a coffee can on the log step.

'Looks real neat,' said Bingo. 'A proper little home.'

'I best sit down,' said Judy. 'I am all worn out.'

TIME FLOATS ON

Time floated on and Judy had her baby without mishap and the mill kept breaking down mysteriously. Bingo got his proof that Crow Kay G. was sabotaging the works one day when the green chain developed a busted cog in its fly-wheel just, as it turned out, in that vicinity where the redhead had been working the previous day. The mill shut down for one hour and no one could figure where the damage was, until the redhead came up from beneath the green chain table, saying, 'A-ha, the trouble is down here in this gash in the cog wheel.' The boss-man slapped him on the back, saying, 'Good work, Crow,' and brought the millwright over to put another one on quickly, but it was clear to Bingo, from the crafty satisfaction on the redhead's face, that the bugger was the culprit.

Bingo said nothing to Judy or anyone else of his thoughts

on the subject but it began to bother him some, this question of right and wrong. What Crow was doing was cheating the mill owners, that was clear; but he was putting money in the workers' pockets and no one could deny that was a true blessing, especially for a family man.

Bingo did bring the issue before Judy, in its general terms.

If a man does wrong, he said to Judy — that is, if he commits *criminal acts* — but those acts serve to put money in deserving pockets — that is, it puts food on table of the poor — then is that act wrong? Is what that man's doing morally reprehensible, is what I mean, and is it morally reprehensible for that otherwise innocent party to take it.

'Good god,' said Judy, 'you are talking with a mouth full of mush. I am worried about your condition, Bingo. I can't make out a word you are saying.'

It is a difficult issue, thought Bingo, who tried to think about it no longer, because it was giving him a headache, with Judy's attitude only making matters worse.

'I wish you would make that baby stop squawling,' he told Judy. 'There is never a minute's peace around here.'

She told him he could go take a walk in the woods. He could go take a flying leap, she told him.

THE SEVEN-ROOM HOUSE

A couple of Indians had built it. One morning, out hunting deer, they had followed a creek trail down to the lower Wichapec.

Quiet, one told the other. I hear something.

They crept up to a knoll and peered through the brush.

Not deer, the other said. What is it?

A white man was down by the creek bed, very busy.

What is he doing? the first Indian asked.

He is digging a hole, the second replied.

It is a very big hole. It is too big to be an animal trap. Shall we tell him?

Sure. Let's tell him.

But the Indians were smarter than that, and remained hidden.

He is taking earth from one place and putting it in another, the first Indian observed.

Yes. As you say, he is digging a hole.

The Indians returned to their own area on the high Wichapec, and dug themselves a similar hole. A few weeks later they again found themselves watching from the same thicket.

He has finished the hole, one said.

Yes, and the hole has filled with water. Perhaps he intends to go swimming.

Then why does he not swim in the creek?

The Indians did not care to dwell further on this.

Why is he notching those logs and stacking them one upon the other?

I believe he is building a wall.

He appears to be building several.

Yes. He intends to erect a square box in which to catch the animals.

It will not work.

Who knows? I have seen stranger things.

The Indians were impressed by what they had seen and went back to their own area on the Wichapec, and duplicated the man's labour. Some time afterwards, they again came down to the creek floor.

Very impressive, the first Indian conceded.

Yes, said the second. He has divided the box into seven different spaces. He has slapped mud between the log walls, and now seems to be putting a cover over it.

It seems very snug, said the first.

Yes, replied the second. It is too bad, isn't it? Someone should have told him.

Yes. Shall we?

But the Indians were too smart for this and went away again and completed their own house, exactly as the man had made his.

Then the winter rains came and the creek swelled and rushed about mightily, and the next time they came down the Wichapec no sign remained of the white man's house, not even the hole.

But the Indians were content with their own great structure high on the Wichapec, and lived in it for many years, with their wives and children and others who thought being so enclosed was not out of keeping.

This was the seven-room house inherited by Crow Kay G.

A BELLYACHEFUL

Things got worse and worse and no one knew which way to turn in the one-room shack where Judy and Bingo lived, with the new little baby squawling 24 hours a day and the other youngan acting like a juvenile delinquent, though not yet two years old, and Bingo knew that at worst he was going to kill Judy or she him, or that at best they'd leave each other or blow out their own brains or go hog-crazy if something wasn't done soon, for they hardly had room enough to breathe and they were plain sick of each other.

'I've had it up to here!' Bingo would shout, and Judy, she'd shout the same.

More and more Bingo brooded on the green-chain man with the red hair and the big seven-room house all to his lonesome. He got to thinking, too, and reminding Judy, of how when he married her she'd weighed in at a sweet 116 pounds — 'and look at you now!' he'd say. 'God, you're big as a moose and about as pretty!' Until these days came along Bingo had never really noticed or paid any attention or much minded her size. If anything, he'd liked it, and if he'd ever heard anyone joking about Judy's size he would have been inclined to say, 'That's right, she's a good handful, but that's how I like it.' But now that attitude and loving was ancient history. Now he'd say: 'You're big as the moon! God knows what it's taking out of my pay-cheque to feed you!'

And Judy would mope or she'd yank up a child under each

arm and stride off into the woods, or she'd go at him with her broom or her pots and pans.

'I am not a dog,' she would say, 'that you can talk to me of how much it costs to feed me.' And she would feel helpless and sick with fury, hatred would spin before her eyes like a ragged ball, and weight that had always felt good and smooth and prideful on her bones now felt like a leaded sinker, felt like something with claws was raking inside her, and mere sight of Bingo would set her to shaking.

'Eat-eat-eat!' he'd say, and she would think: *surely I will kill him. I am going to stomp on him and smush him like the rat he is.*

One night Bingo went to the seven-room house and stood outside in the dark staring at it, hating and cursing the redhead, Crown Kay G., till the bones in his throat ached.

I have got a real bellyacheful, he said.

Next morning he took the boss aside and asked him how come that nasty green chain puller had this big roomy house up the Wichapec when all he and his had was that one-room shack full of squawling youngans.

'Work it out with him,' the boss said. 'Some Indians built that house and it don't belong to Sundown. But I wouldn't reckon on much. When heart was passed out that Crow kid was off chopping wood.'

AN OVERTURE

'How's about it, kid?' asked Bingo.

'Buzz off,' said the redhead. 'Your old brain's gone goat-hair.'

TIME OFF WITHOUT PAY

After being told to buzz off Bingo got so mad at the redhead and at himself and the world in general that he ripped through every log in the yard and through the next truckful that was brought in and in no time at all there wasn't a stump left to be sawed. And it only two o'clock.

'That's it for the day,' said the boss, 'everybody gets the afternoon off without pay.' Then he came up to Bingo and slapped his shoulder, saying: 'That was some sawing. *Gee*-sus!'

The men grumbled at their lost wages and cast malevolent looks at Bingo, and when he passed Crow Kay G. the redhead whispered, 'You're asking for it, saw-dog.'

Bingo said to hell with it and he went home and was sweet to Judy and they hauled up the brats and went flying down the Wichapec to the Lumberjack Bar.

'Keep'm coming,' he told the barkeep.

And for all that they had a roaring good time.

JUDY'S PERCEPTIVE NATURE

'All I could see,' Bingo told Judy, 'while I was sawing them logs was his red eyebrows. I kept thinking of the right and wrong of it and how I had been wronged — how *we* had been wronged — and each time I went zipping through another log I thought, "Well, Crow, you s.o.b., here's another buck out of your pocket."'

'What's his house like?' asked Judy. She was feeding beer to her babies to keep them quiet.

'It's just what you'd expect a couple of Indians to build. But it's been standing for over a hundred years, so I reckon it's solid. But Crow don't need it. He lives in one corner off in the kitchen. He don't have a stick of furniture in the place.'

The juke-box had been going, Mervis Pearl singing *Wreck on the Highway*. The baby had crawled out on the dance floor. Judy told the other child to go dance with her. The boy protested:

'She can't dance. She can't hardly crawl. She barely can sit up.'

'Do what I tell you,' Judy said, and gave him a smack on the bottom. The boy went out, took the baby's hand, and started circling around her.

'Look at that pair,' said Judy. 'Cotton candy wouldn't melt in their mouths.'

54

Bingo, too, was all smiles. 'They are a pretty sight,' he concurred. 'I can't hardly remember the time I was ever innocent and pretty as them.'

Judy slapped playfully at his arm. 'Shoot,' she laughed, 'you still are.'

Mervis went on singing,

> *I saw the wreck on the highway,*
> *but I didn't hear nobody pray* . . . .

Two or three of the lumberjacks were up kicking their heels. Lots of others were yelling encouragement. Everyone was getting high.

'Maybe we should invite that Crow fellow over for a meal,' said Judy. 'Maybe he's lonesome. Maybe when you get to know him he's just as nice as the next guy.'

'Over my grave,' said Bingo.

Judy wriggled out of the booth and coaxed Bingo to dance with her. Bingo put his head on her shoulder. They rocked slowly, off in a corner by themselves, with the youngan tugging at her skirt.

'You are still my sweet one-sixteen,' murmured Bingo at one point. 'You got my number.'

Judy liked that. She let her head sink down, too.

A woman with blonde hair swept high on her head came out of the Ladies and put her arms around them. They embraced her in return and together made several graceless circles of the floor, laughing, for the woman kept losing her balance and toppling against them. She had a tiny red mouth and a green bow up over one ear.

'You two give me hope,' the woman said at the end. 'I got hope in my heart so long as I know there's one loving couple left in the world.' Then she smiled sadly and fluttered her fingers, ta-taing along.

On the drive back up the Wichapec, with the children asleep in her lap, it was determined that (1) Judy would have to do the inviting; (2) it must be a regular dinner, nothing special; (3) they must on no account beg or plead with the redhead to swap houses or offer to pay him a lot of money; (4) she would have to do all of the talking.

'I ought to get a new dress,' mused Judy. 'If I had hair like that blonde woman's I'd be sitting pretty.' She punched Bingo softly in the ribs. 'Now don't deny it. I could see you liked her.'

BIG JUDY AND CROW KAY G.

Early the next morning soon after sunrise Judy crossed through the woods to Crow's big house and knocked on the door. He was a long time answering and when the door was finally opened all he did was look at her. He looked a good long time, until Judy began to get fidgety, and she recognized that he did not know how to talk to strangers.

He did not know how to talk to a woman.

She saw that.

He looked at her with a bottomless, fathomless look that made Judy not know where to look herself. His look set loose all sorts of fast and loose parts inside herself and she did not know what to think. She felt like maybe she was down to 116 pounds again and she scrunched up her toes inside her shoes and swayed a time or two, trying to get hold of herself.

She looked up at the tree-tops and over to the side of the house where there was a big rock, and when she looked back again at him he was still looking.

My, my, she thought — and had the feeling that with wings she could fly right up to the roof or the tree-tops or clean out of the world.

'Bingo and I was thinking,' she said in a light voice, 'we were thinking how you must get terrible lonesome in this big house all alone, and we were wondering if you'd like to come over to our place tonight for potluck supper.'

The redhead didn't reply to this. He had the reddest hair Judy had ever seen and she must have caught him shaving because one side of his face still had the lather.

He had only one boot on, and that half-laced.

'Supper tonight,' she said. 'You coming?'

She saw he did not know how to say 'no' either, or any other word; he seemed straight-out entranced.

'Judy,' she said, extending her hand. 'Judy and Bingo . . . the sawman . . . I'm his other half.'

He blinked at that. But he took her hand and for a minute she thought he was going to kiss it.

She backed down the steps.

'About six,' she said. 'After I've had time to get the shack tidy.'

The redhead kept on looking.

Heading back through the woods, Judy thought: *My, my, he sure can LOOK!* She thought: *If I die tomorrow I know I can go to my grave knowing I have been LOOKED AT once in my life. He has stripped my dress clean off me and seen everything I have.*

Thrilled, is how Judy felt. *Good Lord,* she thought, *and me a married woman. And me with my hair hardly even combed.*

SUPPER AT THE SHACK

Waiting for the meal to get to the table, Bingo saw how Crow Kay G. and Judy kept looking at each other. He saw how Judy was acting flighty and tipsy and how she kept blushing. He saw how the redhead kept staring at her ankles.

But he didn't mind Crow's looking. How he felt about it was that it was a free country. Despite her size, Judy was a good-looking woman. She was a real eyeful.

It was high time she got a little attention.

He just hoped the spaghetti didn't boil over.

SUPPER AT THE SHACK — ANOTHER ANGLE

Crow Kay G., waiting for the meal, saw how, moving about, the sawman and Judy kept bumping into one another and even into him; he saw how the little boy was always at your elbow as he played, and how the baby's squawls were right in your ear, and how the only space she could crawl was down under the table and between your feet and around the chairs; he saw how the bed had been jammed in and how pallets had to be made for the kids, and how, once the spaghetti was cooked and then lobbed out into plates, there was no room on the table for your elbows or for dish or glass, and no way you could scrape your chair back and how you couldn't move without thinking you'd step on the baby, and how when Judy had to change a diaper she had to do it right there in plain sight, and how you had to hold your nose; and how, although it was plenty cold outside, the heat from the cooking on the open barrel made the room so stifling hot you had to take off your jacket, and then no place to put it, and how, even so, a draft came up through the floorboards and froze your ankles, and how pots and pans and all their belongings were stacked all over the room — and how, despite all this, Judy kept the sparkle in her eyes and lit up the place with her sunshine, without one word of complaint.

He frankly couldn't see how human beings could live like this.

I'd die, he thought. I'd sure-as-shooting kill myself.

Midway through the meal the oldest youngan cut his knee from a nail protruding from the wall, and there was much squawling about that.

Then the baby squawled because it wanted to nurse, and the next course never did come. But Crow didn't mind, for the sawman had out his jug.

Crow, from time to time, kept trying to get a bead on the saw-dog — on how a woman like Judy could be hooked up with a snake like that — but he couldn't get anywhere. He couldn't figure it out. This Bingo character, it seemed to him, was a born Nothing. Real Low-life.

'I hear tell,' said Bingo of a sudden, 'that big house of yours was built by Indians.'

Crow cautiously nodded.

'Must be hard for you,' said Bingo, 'keeping up a big house like that. The heat bill alone must keep your pocket-book empty.'

58

'I manage,' said the redhead. He thought it best not to tell the saw-dog that he had shut off the rooms and now lived entirely in the kitchen.

'Now if you'd want to trade abodes,' Bingo trailed on, 'I wouldn't mind — Judy and me wouldn't — sweetening the pot. To make it worth your while.'

Crow remained silent. He was watching Judy burp the baby. Then he watched her button up her blouse. He watched her laugh and spin her hands as if she were chasing away flies.

'I declare,' she said, 'all Bingo Duncan has to do is look at me and I'm pregnant again.'

Bingo let out a sound, half-groan and half-surprise. He gazed searchingly at Judy. He clearly was wondering whether she was telling him a third child was in the oven.

Shortly after this, Crow Kay G. departed. He left with mixed feelings, not quite wanting to go but thinking he'd best move fast, for in truth he found the evening confusing. He couldn't figure out what to make of all those signals he had been getting — nor even from where they had been coming.

'That Judy,' he exclaimed to the air, 'now *that's* a woman.'

The night wind was invigorating, however, and by the time he arrived at the house the Indians had built, he felt again half-normal. He entered the back door with grand satisfaction, and before going to bed strolled through each of the seven rooms, delighted they were all of them his.

CLEANING UP FROM DINNER

'Well, we blew that,' said Bingo. 'We can say goodby to that idea.'

'Like I said,' said Judy, 'it's too early to count chickens.'

IN BED THAT NIGHT

I feel *this* light-headed! said Judy. I feel a small breeze could blow me straight up to the tree-tops.

What was that about an oven? said Bingo.

Stop talking, said the youngan. How can I sleep with your yakking going on?

Put your arms around me, Bingo. Hold me tight. Or I'll float on out of here.

Where would we put another one? asked Bingo. How we going to feed another one? What's the percentage?

One little gust and I'm gone, said Judy, trembling.

Bingo put his arms, and one leg, around her. She held on tight.

The boy stayed quiet. He had the feeling something strange was going on. He didn't move a muscle.

The baby was sleeping.

When tomorrow comes, said Judy, I hope I'm back down to earth.

I'm getting woozy up here.

THE CUP OF COFFEE

Lunch-time the next day when the mill shut down there were only a few logs in the yard and they all knew no more trucks were bringing in logs that day and they were uneasy; talk was circulating to the effect that the mill was going to close down for good now, Sundown was going to call it quits, and some were passing along the rumour that the company wouldn't even be able to pay them for the week already put in.

Crow Kay G. sat over on the 2 x 8 stack by the green chain, eating a tomato sandwich. The bread had gone soggy and he didn't much like it.

Bingo came over and sat down beside him. He had two or three roast beef sandwiches in his lunch-pail, together with a wedge of cake, a carrot, and a red apple. He had a large thermosful of hot coffee as well.

You think they gonna shut down? Bingo asked.

Crow shook his head, not yes, not no.

C'est la vie, he said.

Bingo ate his lunch and drank his coffee. The day was a cold one and he held his hands over the steaming cup, for warmth.

I see she looks after you real good, said Crow. I see she packs a man's lunch.

Who? asked Bingo.

Your wife. That Judith.

REFLECTING ON THAT

Just as they had figured, the mill did not start back up after lunch, though there was word more logs would be coming in in the morning. Walking back to his shack, swinging the empty lunch-pail, Bingo had mind to reflect back on those minutes by the green chain. *Judith,* he thought . . . *well, I'll be damned. That IS her name. I'd plumb forgot about it. Little Judith, that is exactly what I used to call her.*

HISTORY REPEATED

As Bingo walked through the door, Judy asked, 'Did you?'

'Did I what?'

'Bingo Duncan, don't tell me you forgot!'

Bingo hemmed and hawed. Finally, he said: 'We had a lot of other stuff to talk about. I guess it slipped my mind. Anyway, it is his turn to ask us.'

But Judy would have none of that, so fast as she could she went running over to ask Crow Kay G. if he wanted to come over tonight for meat and mashed potatoes.

She shortly returned, looking downcast, explaining: He could not come. He was on his way down to the beach to cut grape stakes. He says he sells them for thirty, thirty-five cents to the grape and berry people down south. It is clear he is an Up-and-Go-Getter. Why did you not ever think of that for making extra money?

Bingo sighed. He said he was tired. He said the one thing in the world he wanted right now was a nice easy chair to sit down in.

'If you'd thought of cutting stakes like that redhead,' Judy said, 'maybe we'd have one. Maybe we'd have us a seven-room house, too.'

Bingo went out and sat on a stump in the cleared space out

back. He was in no mood to hear anymore about the world's Go-Getters.

'He said he'd stop by on his way home,' called Judy, 'if our light was on.'

THE LIGHT, AND CROW AND THE YOUNGAN, AND JUDY ALONE WITH HER THOUGHTS

Each time Bingo turned off the light Judy came by and turned it back on.

'One would think you were taken with this fella,' said Bingo.

'Don't be silly,' she said. 'You may not have noticed, but your oldest child is not home.'

'Good God! Where is he?'

'He is out grape-stacking with Crow. He asked if he could, and I let'm.'

About midnight the child came in, very excited, with his pant legs wet.

'We cut 78 stakes!' the youngan exclaimed. 'That's over 30 dollars!'

'Why didn't Mr. Crow come in?' asked Judy.

'He said his ass was slinged, he had to get home to bed.'

Judy asked the youngan if he was hungry. She said, 'Child, you must be starved.'

But the boy was already dropping down on his pallet. 'Not me,' he said. 'We had us three cans of potted meat, down on the beach.'

'I didn't think you liked potted meat.'

'I do now. Crow has got a whole room full. He says it's about all he eats. Do you know what else he has? He has one of those old oil drums cut open with a velvet seat half-way up, and a red canopy over the top. He says he sits in it when he wants to think about his kingdom.'

Judy shook her head, marvelling.

Soon the child fell asleep, and Bingo with him. For a long time after the shack had settled Judy stood at her dark window, looking up at the stars. Alone with her thoughts.

For three days running, four if one counts Sunday, the Sundown mill stayed shut down, and each day the youngan went out with Crow to cut stakes.

I hope he pays you, said Bingo. Then we all can retire.

The fourth day Judy went herself to bring the boy home, for he had been sleeping over, and while at the big house she told Crow Kay G. how she had beard Bingo say that the way to cut stakes was to buy or borrow a chain-saw so you could go at the really big logs and how if you did that you could cut tons more stakes than you could with an axe and chisel.

'What we need is a Jeep,' said Crow. 'With a Jeep we could zip up and down the beach without getting stuck in the sand. We could hunt out the really big logs.'

'I will ask him where we can get a Jeep,' said Judy.

He was not coming over to dinner that night, but then he said he would.

Judy perked up.

Wonder what changed his mind? thought Judy. Wonder has he been missing me? Maybe it was my saying all Bingo had to do was look at me and I'd be pregnant again.

Maybe he's jealous.

She jumped her way home, happy as a kid, uplifted by that.

CUTTING STAKES ON THE BEACH

The next weekend Bingo had the power-saw and the Jeep and they drove down to the beach and looked about for a huge, washed-up redwood and when they found one they got out and sawed it into sections eight feet long like the growers wanted, and with the axes and chisels they split these into two- to three-inch stakes and chopped the point on their tips so the growers could drive them into the ground. While the men worked Judy and the kids zoomed up and down the beach in the Jeep and sometimes Judy drove the Jeep into the water where the water and sand were swirling together, and the tires kicked up a splash and spun deep into the sand and she drove the Jeep very fast and snake-zithered against the waves which shot up a fine spray over the Jeep and made the baby and all of them cackle with laughter.

End of the first few weeks they had collected themselves over three hundred dollars.

POPCORN

One night after splitting stakes and roasting weiners on the beach they were driving through Orick when they saw on the movie marquee that what was playing was a movie called

LADY GODIVA & THE LONE RANGER

and when Judy saw this she said, 'Whoops, just what I want, a big bag of popcorn!'

THE LUMBERJACK BAR

Where they were going was the Lumberjack Bar, and Judy brought her popcorn with her, and they took a booth in the back near the juke-box.

I want to dance-dance-dance, said Judy, and she danced first with Bingo, then with Crow, and then she danced with the baby wiggling in her arms and the other youngan swinging on her skirt. One of her old friends from the All Nite Highway Cafe, sauntering by, said, Well, darling, I see you're still dancing, and Judy said, Yes I thought I'd best get it out of my system while I can, for I've up and got pregnant again.

Meantime, Bingo and Crow were back in the booth drinking their beers, paying no attention to the conversation of two loggers, a skinner and a faller, seated near to them.

The Skinner: 'Now here, now there. Not anywhere.'

The Faller: 'I ain't telling, but the bastard stole my shirt.'

The Skinner: 'Flipped right over the canyon, bottom-side up, and when I got down to him the sonofabitch was sitting up on the frame, grinning his head off.'

The Faller: 'Speaking of fire, that was her to a tee. So hot she burned holes in my blankets.'

Bingo wiped wet circles on the formica. 'What the hell are those two bull-shooters talking about?' he asked Crow.

But the redhead was not feeling talkative. Sure, he could split stakes alongside this character, and drive up and down the Wichapec with him. Sure, they were partners, but still there was something about this saw-dog that rubbed him wrong, and he didn't see why he had to sit here shooting the breeze with him.

What he wanted to do was go dance with Judy.

But it looked to him like the children had her all tied up.

'Let's have another beer,' he said. 'Let's tie one on.'

A blonde woman with piled-up hair approached and stood grinning beside their booth. Then she slipped in beside Bingo, and slung an arm around him, saying, 'Hi, honey. Long time no see.'

The redhead watched this with an open mouth. Sonofagun, he thought, this character has been running around on Judy. And me staying pure as the snow.

He got up and went outside and sat in the Jeep, banging his fist on the steering wheel.

THE ETERNAL QUESTION

Was he or wasn't he, that was the eternal question plaguing Judy, once Crow Kay G. first hinted at it and then said his suspicions straight out. She took to searching his pockets for phone numbers and looking over his shirts for lipstick stains and his drawers for you-know-what.

What's the matter with you? Bingo would say.

For Judy had stopped eating, too, and anytime he was out of her sight for a second she would be calling his name, and some days she would walk up to the mill just to make sure he was seated in his sawyer's chair.

'I believe he's innocent,' she told Crow one day.

Another day she did find a telephone number scrawled on

65

a sheet in his pocket, but when she asked him about it he said it was some fella he'd heard of who had a dog for sale and he was thinking of buying a dog.

'Don't lie to me, Bingo. I bet it's that blonde woman's number.'

But when she called an old rasping voice said, 'Hell's fire, lady, you're the second caller I've had this week. I sold that dog more than a month ago.'

Not that Judy was convinced.

FAMILY CHANGES

One morning Judy went up to the seven-room house and opened all the doors, aired the rooms, swept up the dust and cobwebs, washed the windows, and that night told Bingo it was as pretty a place as she'd ever seen. It was like heaven.

'Them Indians really knew what they were doing,' she said.

A few days later they rushed her down the mountain and Judy gave birth to their newest baby.

'That tears it,' said Bingo. 'We can't all live in that shack now.'

While Bingo was down overseeing Judy's condition in the hospital the oldest youngan had taken to staying over nights at the redhead's house. For several days Bingo hardly even saw him.

'I guess I could build another room on to the shack,' Bingo told Judy. 'Maybe that's one solution.'

Judy objected. 'You think I'm going to come home to your sawing and pounding? You think I would make our baby live like that?'

'It's all I can think of. One thing for sure, we can't all put up in that one little room.'

Crow, standing out in the hospital corridor, ventured in. 'She could put up with me,' he said. 'While you're building. Judy and the baby. I wouldn't mind having them.'

THE DREAM

That night Bingo had one of his worst dreams. He waked

up sweating. What had happened was that the saw seat had warped under him and dropped him off backwards into the log chute and he'd been carried right along the belt, tumbling over midst the bark and slivers and chunks of wood, and try as he could he couldn't get upright again. Then he'd got scrambled around between the green chain hooks and the chains carrying scrap up the waste chute to drop it off in the cone burner, and first thing he knew that was what had him. He was on his way to being burned alive. Up ahead were flames licking from the burner, and the chains kept tumbling him over, wood chunks knocking him one way and the other and his arms and legs gone all twisty. And knowing he was finished, he had done a strange thing: he had started calling for his mama. *Mama, help me!* — that's what he'd screeched out. But what part of the dream his mama might have occupied was all dark and mystery and he knew there was no help there. He could feel the heat of the burner. Could see the red flames. And he made one last effort to stand — one last claim that his life was not yet over. Up that high, his clothes already catching afire, he had a clear view of the Wichapec before him. Down there was the one-room shack with nobody in it, and up there was the redhead's place, glaring bright as a mansion, and, yes, there stood Judy waving her arms from the front door, screaming in a silent way, '*Jump! Jump! Jump!*' And the funny thing about it to his mind was how Judy had skinned down to her old weight of 116, how she looked pretty as a picture, even as — when he looked twice — his kids were climbing all over her. Kids running through her like a fast-growth vine. Funny thing to him was how beautiful she looked. How clean and simple and next to ravishing. Just the way she would look — would stay looking — if she'd never hooked up with him. The other funny thing was how Crow Kay G. was absent. How he wasn't where you'd think to find him. Not up at the house with his arms around Judy, nor down there by the sawyer's seat waving a wrench, saying 'Look what I done. Look how I fixed your goose.' No, Crow was nowhere to be seen. Then

Bingo nodded yes it was.

Crow Kay G. got the kids assembled for a ride in the Jeep. He asked Judy if she'd care to come along.

'I reckon so,' she said, 'as no one around here will talk to me.'

Bingo threw more driftwood on. He sat poking the fire, talking this and that to the baby, as the others roared in the Jeep down the beach, swerving into and out of the waves.

Tonight Crow had brought his pistol along and as he burst across the dunes he would rest his pistol wrist over his driving arm and take pot-shots at dark shapes as they surfaced far out in the water.

'What are you shooting at?' asked Judy.

'Sea-lions,' said Crow. 'The ocean is packed full with them.'

They drove as far as they could down the stretch of sand and when they came back, more slowly now because it seemed something had gone out of each of them, they saw dead black shapes washing up on the tide.

'What's those?' asked Judy.

'Sea-lions,' Crow said.

HORSEMAN, PASS BY

First the youngan came in.

Then the toddler.

Bingo, stretched out on the bed with the year-old copy of a book found between the floorboards — *Eccentric Millionaires* — watched the black entrance to see who next would come.

Judy's voice, outside in the dark, summoned him forth.

'I'm home,' she said, 'for anyone who can carry me over the threshold!'

THIRTY YEARS LATER

'Well, tell me, Bingo,' Judy would say, 'was it worth it?'

'Sit down,' Bingo would say. 'I am going to sing you a love song.'

'But will it be pretty?'

'It will be a honey.'

And she would sit down, patting her feet, and he would do it.

Nine children and nineteen grandchildren, she'd think, and I don't feel a day over forty.

Then they'd go to bed where, to her mind and his, every time it was like starting over.

A Nicer Story
by the 'B' Road

IN MY HIGH SCHOOL Agnes was the tallest and the fattest girl around, and the one most feared. She had three eyes high in her forehead, each looking off in different directions so we could never slip up on her and get even. She had hands like a meat-axe and liked chopping off our necks. 'Yah, you blimp, you dreg!' we'd taunt — and she'd chase us down and sit on us because she was also the fastest and the most brutal.

'Stop whimpering, you little squirt' she'd say, 'or I'll take off your pants.'

The other thing is Agnes had money. She'd come to school each day with a brand-new twenty dollar bill tucked up under her chin, saying, 'If you can take it, it's yours.'

Nobody ever took it. Death wasn't worth it.

For Agnes dearly loved her money.

In the fall she went out for the football team and survived all cuts. In the first game she ran for 296 yards, scored nine touchdowns and threw for seven others. She kicked four field goals. She played tackle on defence and put three guys in the hospital. And through it all she never even breathed hard or got her nails dirty.

We beat Wilfrid Laurier 124 to nothing and I never got in the game.

When it was over the coach approached her, grinning, his hand outstretched: 'Great game, kid,' he said, 'this year the trophy's ours for sure!'

Agnes peeled off her helmet.

'You can shove it,' she told him. 'What do you think I am, a moron? I hate it! It's stupid! This is the dumbest game I ever played! I quit!'

'Quit!' gasped the coach. 'My God, you can't —'

'Anyway,' said Agnes, striding on, 'I'm a girl. The gridiron is no place for the fair sex.' But stopping there by the midfield stripe to tell him this: 'And I don't like *you* either. I don't like how you make these little jerks dance to your caterwauling and how they swoon over themselves in their pads and I hate how you're always tooting your stupid little whistle. Christ, it all makes me sick!' Rooting under her jersey and wriggling out of her shoulder pads and tugging them down through her sleeve, all to drop them at her feet so they could lie enfeebled there under the floodlights like the bleached upturned bones of some ghostly reptilian creature. 'All I like about it,' she said, 'only reason I've stuck it out and played your silly game, is how the people in the stands clap and cheer, how they flash their boaty smiles and slap shoulders, how they rock the bleachers and go home together singing. They got so little to cheer about in this sock-sucking town I'm pleased I could oblige. But it's a cheap thrill and always at another's expense and I'm plumb sick of it. So what I say is stuff it, coach.'

What a hothead Agnes was.

The coach retired a few seasons later, after 27 consecutive defeats. 'I was never the same after that night,' he told the press. 'The little lady took my starch right out. The old killer instinct just went kaput.'

Agnes had another talent while in high school. She was extremely religious. She had a very liberated sense of what God looked like and how he should conduct himself. Whenever God saw Agnes he was all smiles. Very gracious. He had a long red beard, with fish bones stuck into it for good luck, and with Agnes he was more than cozy. 'How're you doing, Aggie!' he'd say, and his belly-booming voice would sway the tree-tops and go rumbling like an ox-cart through pasture, rock, and town.

He'd throw a fat arm around her shoulders, laughing, and drop gold coins into her hands.

They'd walk off together into the moonlight, and sooner or later, our side pitched into utter darkness, we'd see a great fiery mass of light churning up over the other side of town, illuminating roof-top and smoke-stack and every inch of the distant, wavy, horizon.

'Where were you last night?' I'd ask her.

'Don't get personal,' she'd say.

But I'd see that blush on her skin and how her hips pressed out and how she walked with a certain timid regard for how her feet might or might not touch down — and was able to put two and two together.

'Well,' I'd snarl, 'I hope you enjoyed yourself.'

'It was just peachy.'

In the spring of our next-to-final year Agnes dropped out of school — something about a watch missing from some joker's locker — and she disappeared. *Splatt,* right off the face of the earth. I didn't see her again for fourteen years.

Just a few days ago this was. I turned a corner down on Yonge Street — just up from Wheels 'N Flags 'N Things, the kid's store, where I'd been in chatting with the owner about a new scoop-shovel idea — and there was Agnes coming directly towards me.

My, my, how she'd changed.

'Mervis!' she said — 'as I live and breathe!'

And I said pretty much the same.

'You look fine, Agnes. Really fine.'

'Yes,' she said, brushing aside the compliment. 'None the worse for wear, I suppose. But you, Mervis? How's life treating you?'

I brought her up to date. 'I'm married now,' I told her, 'to a nine-foot goddess with gold teeth and a watch chain made out of links from a cyclone fence. But don't get the idea it isn't old Mervis who rules the roost! We've got nineteen children between us and last year I cleared two hundred thousand after tax.'

'Goodness,' said Agnes, 'you're doing almost as well as I am.'

We decided to stop off at The Courtyard Cafe to talk about it.

'So what are you into?' I asked, once the waiter had placed down the celebratory champagne in a gleaming silver bucket.

'I'm God's wife,' she said happily. 'And it truly is wonderful. I've got a thousand joys out of life I never dreamed could be mine for the asking back there during our old days at Northern Secondary.

'It's the travel, though,' she said, gripping the white tablecloth. 'God, it gets tedious running all over the universe and never quite knowing why!' She reared back, glugging down her champagne. 'Christ, this is good!'

Our knees touched under the table.

'There's something I never told you, Agnes,' I said, 'getting back to our wild old days at high school.'

'What's that, honey?'

'I was always a little envious of you. A little afraid. You always made the rest of us feel like such pathetic worms.'

'But how dreadful! Surely you can't mean that, Mervis.'

'And do you remember the football team? We lost twenty-seven straight.'

'Yes?'

'I sat on the bench the whole time. Three long seasons the coach never let me into a single game.'

'How awful! But surely you can't blame me. I was long gone by then.'

'If you saw all those games as one game we would have lost it thirteen hundred eighty seven to one twenty-four. And I never checked in even for a second.'

'I can see what you mean. Being a benchwarmer is certainly no fun. And I can see too that no matter what success life eventually brings it's the benchwarming feeling that always sticks. But what the hell, Mervis, why blame me just because you couldn't cut it?'

'I'm not blaming you.'

'Yes you are.'

The waiter slipped in and topped my glass.

'The hell I am.'

'You are, Mervis. You've got the same old whine in your voice now that you had then.'

I let that pass.

'I'll tell you something else, Agnes,' I said. 'You were never liked at school. We all sighed sighs of joy when you disappeared.'

Agnes smiled her old impervious smile.

'*You* never liked me, Mervis. *You* sighed sighs of joy.'

'That's a lie, Agnes. You scared me, you had me spinning for a while. But I always carried around a soft spot for you.'

'Perhaps so. I remember a stroll we had one night in the moonlight. You had a lot to say to me that night, as I recall. But you were going with some little drip of a girl at the time, some nasty little dodge-baller who was forever jabbing her finger into your chest. What became of that bossy little number?'

'Little Mirabel, you mean?'

'She's the one. None of us could ever figure out what you saw in her.'

It wasn't what she said but the mocking, arrogant gleam in her eyes that made me do what I next did.

'Here's a new twenty under my chin, Agnes,' I said. 'If you can yank it out it's yours.'

Before I'd even got my hands back on the table she'd reached over and grabbed the twenty from beneath my chin and dropped it down her dress.

'You're slow, Mervis,' she said. 'So slow. You always were. I could pick my teeth with what you have for brains.'

A desire for simple, uncluttered justice came over me. I can't explain it any other way. I picked up the champagne bottle and without another thought slammed it against her beautiful head. The bottle burst, sending glass and foam everywhere.

Five or six people screamed.

'Why'd you do that?' sobbed Agnes, slumping down between the tables.

'Revenge is wonderful, Agnes,' I said. 'I always knew that one day, for sake of my own mental health, I was going to have to get even.'

'Well, you've done it, Mervis,' she said. 'I think you've killed me.'

'It was writ in the stars, Agnes. It was writ a long time ago.'

'It *hurts*, Mervis!' she cried. 'I solemnly hurt all over.'

Funny thing was, I didn't feel any elation. What I felt was *strange*. Just damned *peculiar*. *Weird*, if you want to know the truth. As if I now found myself on the *other side* of my life, looking back at it through some craggy woeful knot-hole, and hardly recognizing myself. There I was, for instance, sitting on a long bench with a bucket between my legs. Alone. All suited up. And the coach stabbing a finger my way, shouting *'Get in there, boy! Give them the old Northern*

She picked herself up and began rubbing her head.

'That wasn't nice, Mervis,' she complained. 'You could hurt someone that way. You really ought to avail yourself of professional counsel.'

I dropped down into my chair, wringing my hands. *No one* could ever beat Agnes.

She picked tiny shards of glass out of her hair, arranging them in a neat pile on the table. 'Have you tried *curbing* those impulses, Mervis? Really *tried*? Don't you know *yet* that people are nicer to you when you're nice to them?'

'I was nice to the coach,' I said. 'I really buttered him up. *Still* I never got into the game.'

'I didn't say it worked for everyone, Mervis.'

I moaned. Agnes had always had a way of complicating *everything*.

'It wasn't right,' I said. 'I could have won some of those games.'

'I'm sure you could have. I remember how fleet-footed you were, running through *kick-in-the-pants!'* And the bleachers were roaring 'GO, MERVIS, GO!' But it wasn't me that went scooting in. I couldn't. I was hunkered over on the bench with my feet in the bucket and my helmet jammed down over my eyes, crying *'Oh, coach, give me a chance!'* And a moment later a swirl of hats rising over the grandstand, everyone yelling 'TOUCHDOWN! TOUCHDOWN! YEA, MIRABEL!' Then the stadium empty and black and my little knot-hole closing. Slowly opening up to my other eye. There I was again, this time loping off into the moonlight with Agnes at my side. Agnes taunting, saying *'Come on, Mervis, show me what you've got between those two legs.'* Only what Agnes was truly saying, when I got up close, was 'Mervis, get your sock-sucking hands off me! Mervis now Mervis don't you dare!' For I was up on top of her and squirming to get her legs open. Agnes screaming 'MERVIS MERVIS HAVE YOU LOST YOUR

the tires during training. You had the highest knees around.'

'It was your fault, Agnes. The coach figured if one girl could get the job done then another could. He kept suiting up the females, zipping them in and out of the games. Even Mirabel made the team. First-string. And do you think she ever let me forget it? No, every day for twenty years that's all I've heard. About how she tackled this guy and put the knee in that one and knocked the stuffings out of a thousand others, and what a good broken-field runner she was when she got the ball.'

'That little chest-thumper! You married *her*? Oh, Mervis, I'm sorry!'

'It was Mirabel or nothing, Agnes, after you disappeared.'

'We'd best not go into that, Mervis.'

'Why not? I've nothing to hide.'

'Let's not go into it, Mervis.'

'If you say so. But no need to get so secretive and hurt

MIND?' Agnes clawing away from me. Agnes kicking, beating my head and shoulders, crying 'MERVIS PLEASE!' No, not my shoulders. Because in fact it wasn't me. Not anyone remotely *like* me. Who it was was some raspy, pimply creature who picked up a stone and hit her, kept hitting her on the head. Five or six people screaming too, just screaming, but there was nothing they could do about it. *Splatt*, and it was all over, with leaves blowing up to cover her and the knot-hole slamming shut. Not Mervis. Not me. I was sweaty-hot, I was wilty, but I knew that much. Mervis is innocent as day-old cheese. Mervis is straight in the heart and mind, he is totally without guile. Funny thing, though.

The people were still screaming. Some five or six. And tables over-turning, dishes and cutlery clattering, shapes rushing by. Bedlam. Agnes deathly still on the floor. I took the white towel out of the bucket, meaning to place it over her bleeding head. To cover her up. No, not to cover her up. That's

about it. No need to get so woe-eyed accusatory about it.'

'It did *hurt*, Mervis. It hurts everytime I rub my head or find myself looking back, thinking of it.'

'Yeah, *you*. Nothing ever hurt you. You were always walking off into the moonlight with God, leading him by the hand.'

'I had my own life to lead, thank you, Mervis.'

'And you led it. You let him do whatever he wanted to do with you. The nights I stood out alone in my little scrub-grass yard watching half the sky light up with what the two of you were doing. It was sickening. I would throw up everytime I saw the sky go red.'

'You've a nasty mind, Mervis. Anyway, God and I had a lot to give each other. To give to each other and to others too. You'd have known that had you not been so all-fiery stupid in your head, such a chiseler, with your mean little mind and your heart the size of a peach pit.'

'Mirabel liked me all right.'

'Two of a kind, Mervis.'

nonsense. Why would I want to cover her up? How silly! But all those people were screaming — well, they had been — getting me confused. Very unlike me to react that way. Really curious. Well, one never knows. I mean, disaster strikes, what's one to do? So I knelt down beside her, intending to do what I could. To help her out, if help I could. Brush the glass out of her face. Arrange her hair. Yet! — funny thing! Really most curious. Mind-boggling, to tell the truth. For once I began tending her it became gradually clear to me that *this was not Agnes*! Radiantly clear. But who was it? She looked familiar somehow. Stranger yet — most bizarre! — she looked faintly like Mirabel. Had her puckered nose. Christ help me, it *was* Mirabel. Poor Mirabel.

'Mirabel,' I said, taking her head into my lap, 'how did *you* get here. Speak to me Mirabel.'

But her eyes went on past me. Her eyes were soft now, and yielding now, now that they saw nothing.

I sobbed, and clutched her

'Yeah, what do you know about it? We didn't all have your advantages, you know. We didn't all have God there to swing the big deals, to drop gold coins into our hands, to go marching us off into the moonlight.'

'You never cared for the moonlight, Mervis. For you the moonlight was no more than a place where you could bash people over the head with rocks and know you wouldn't be seen.'

'Rubbish. You talk like I was some kind of criminal.'

'You are, Mervis.'

'Well, I've covered that up. None of that old business bothers me any more.'

'I know, Mervis. You are a very sweet man. A very decent man. Or would have been, had no one ever asked anything of you, never expected anything of you.'

'I invented a new kind of scoop-shovel the other day. It's going to make me a million bucks.'

'It fits, darling. Cover everything up.'

'How's your head?'

'It's fine now, thank you. Shall we go?'

'Who's to pay the bill?'

to me. A policeman took my arm. He kept yanking me. Kept whispering in my ear. 'If you're smart, you'll say nothing. Not a blessed word. You hear me? I see these domestic squabbles ten times a day. You have words, one word leads to another, you get hit, you hit back, slap a person around — sooner or later someone gets hurt. Isn't that how it is? What was the little spitfire doing, playing around? You caught her out? She caught *you* out? Forget that, forget I asked. Don't want to know. If you're smart you'll keep your yap shut. Admit to nothing. Hell, where's the proof? These people, they were eating their dinner, they saw nothing. In this day and age, everybody out to get you, a guy has got to keep his wits. You dig?' I told him I did.

'Right,' he said, 'you get on home now. Try not to panic. I see guys like you every day, you're found out for one crime you'll admit to a thousand others.'

'There was this case back in high school,' I said. 'Something about a missing person.'

'I will, sweetheart. I always do.'

She pulled my twenty out of her dress and held it high; we watched it flutter down to the white table-cloth. We said our goodbys out on the street in front of the Windsor Arms.

'It *is* depressing, Mervis, that you always want *to* hurt me so. You should think about that. Try to make amends,' she said.

'Maybe,' I said. 'Maybe I will.'

'And give funny little Mirabel a chance. Could be it's all she needs.'

'Could be,' I said. 'So long. Take care of yourself.'

'Poor Mervis,' she smiled. She tilted up on her heels and settled a hot, moist kiss on my mouth.

It was heaven.

Agnes, I realized, had changed over the long hang of years since I'd seen her last. She'd become — forgiving!

'I forgive you that business with the watch too, Mervis. Truth is, I'm a very forgiving sort.'

'I don't remember anything about a watch, Agnes.'

'Don't want to hear about it,' he said. 'Not my neighbourhood.'

'And there was this report put in on a stolen watch.'

'Ancient history. Now move along. Take a taxi, get off the street.'

'I do *try* to learn,' I told her. 'I'm not so dense as you think.'

'I know. That's why I bother with you.'

'No hard feelings?'

'None.'

I watched her jump into a taxi and steal away.

I came on back home.

Cleared out the place, wiped up all my prints.

Did a good job, too. You'd never believe anyone had ever lived in this dump.

Went down to the lobby, watched a little TV. Not much doing on *any* of the channels. No late-breaking news. Everything *too* quiet, in fact.

Wept over Mirabel. She'd had her easier side, come sunny days. Not a bad woman, to tell the truth, if she hadn't forever been poking her finger into my chest.

'Do this, do that!' Drives a body crazy.

That Agnes! — quite a
lady, when all was told.

Went back upstairs. Still
had a lot of evidence to
remove.

Mirabel's shoes, for
instance. Christ, she had five
thousand pairs. And hats!
Good lord, how she'd doted
on hats.

No trouble, however. I
pitched them out the win-
dow. Whirled like frisbies, a
lot of fun. People kept running off with them. 'You
throwing anything else
away?' they asked. Nope,
nothing else.

The watch, though, ought
to do something with it.

Give it to Mirabel's old
Daddy, maybe, he'd appre-
ciate it.

Kept good time.

Once or twice heard
someone coming up the
stairs. Thought it was the
police, thought it was Mirabel.

Don't know why I thought that.

Thought if I'd eat some-
thing I might feel better. Had
a good stiff drink instead.

Felt *much* better.

In fact, after a while, felt
wonderful. Felt all the ugli-
ness draining away. Felt
*re*born.

Strangest goddamn feeling
in the world.

Felt I'd *dreamed* this entire
business. That I could do
anything! Mervis the Splendid!
Mervis the Irreproachable!
The Magnificent Mervis!

                          Zip!
    Zap!
                                Zip!
         Zip Zap Zip!

             Zooooooooomm!

             TOUCHDOWN!!!

Why Agnes Left

THE WOMAN WITH NO HAIR has gone home. The body stocking woman has gone home. Agnes has gone. Everyone has gone home and so should I.

You should go home, my hostess Sulvie tells me. What are you waiting for? Everyone left hours ago, and Zephyr and I would like to get some sleep.

Zephyr adds her two cents.

The place is all cleaned up, no one would ever guess that a few short hours ago twenty-seven women were here talking, laughing, having a gay old time.

The place *looks* empty. Its emptiness has permeated my bones, brought me close to tears. It reminds me of a play on closing night when all the beautiful walls come down. Vanishing life. There and then gone.

Zephyr's two cents amount to this:

You should go home, Mr. Banks. We don't know you all this well and in any event Sulvie and I don't allow men to stay overnight.

It isn't that so much, says Sulvie. We have no place to put you. The sofa isn't at all comfortable. You'd catch a cold sleeping on the floor.

Yes, says Zephyr. You'll have to go. Please leave.

It's true, I really must. I have no right to inflict my presence on these two no-nonsense, straightforward women.

Zephyr stands with my overcoat held high to receive my arms. Sulvie extends my hat. I slip my arms into the coat and button up. I put on the hat. A moment later, however — I can't explain it — I am again sitting down.

One more cigarette, I say. Let me finish this and I promise I'll get out of your hair.

Zephyr explodes. *God!* — and stalks off to slam a door.

Sulvie, too, is no longer content to reason with me. *Get out!* she all but screams. My patience is exhausted! Get out this minute!

I drag on the cigarette. They have removed all the ashtrays and I have to thump my ashes into the palm of my hand.

It was a lovely party, I tell her. One of the best I've been to in years.

She smoulders.

I'm amazed that you two could so quickly clean up the place. What a lot of mess!

She mushes a pillow into a chair. I'm not talking to you, Mr. Banks. We have asked you nicely to leave. You refuse. You don't frighten us, if that's what you're thinking. Not at all. You have about five seconds, then Zephyr and I are going to physically throw you out.

No need for that, I say. Just let me have this last cigarette.

You said that an hour ago.

Was it really that long?

Her nostrils flare. Her face has changed colour, gone a deep red.

Zephyr re-enters, drawing the cord on a long blue velvet robe. She has very pretty feet, I notice.

I've called the police, she announces. If you want to avoid spending the night in jail you'd best pack yourself off this minute.

Sulvie has decided to cry. Zephyr tells her to stop snivelling, there is absolutely nothing to warrant tears. I am an oaf, she tells her, but I will be gone soon.

She's only tired, I say. She will feel better in a minute.

They glare at me. Both women have spent all day preparing for the party, no doubt, and they are obviously exhausted.

I am, too, for that matter. I must be. Otherwise, I would not find myself in this awkward situation.

My palm is quite full of ashes. I look about for a place to

put them. The two women watch. Zephyr taps her foot. They are quite certain my ashes shall at any second despoil their vacuumed sky blue carpet.

I slide the ashes into my side pocket. I pinch out the cigarette and drop it inside as well.

You're finished, Zephyr says. She opens the door and stands beside it.

Just let me wipe my hands, I say. I stand. Would it trouble you too much, I ask, if I had a glass of water?

Sulvie screams. Zephyr rushes over to comfort her.

I go in and draw a glass of water from the kitchen tap. Dishes are piled up on the drain-board. The counter and the twin sinks have been wiped clean. The entire kitchen sparkles.

Suddenly Zephyr is behind me, asking what I think I am doing.

Oh, I thought I'd help out, I say. Put away a few dishes, the two of you have worked so hard. It was a lovely dinner you served, by the way. Don't know if I mentioned it before.

Zephyr snatches a golden serving tray from my hand. *Out!* she yells. *Get out of here!* The dish clatters down.

Sorry, I say. Didn't mean to offend.

I thump out another cigarette, heading out into the living-room in front of her.

Sulvie, on the sofa, has her head buried under several pillows. I flop down into the nearest chair.

Won't be a second, I say. Just let me finish this.

Sulvie looks up, is horrified, then again buries her head. Zephyr leans against the sofa back, snarling to herself.

Go on with whatever it is you have to do, I suggest. Don't mind me.

Neither replies.

I make a stab at explaining this business of the cigarette. When I was very young, I tell them, I made a vow to myself never to smoke on the streets. A lot of people do, I think. At home, driving, at a restaurant, at these places okay, but never on the street. It's one way of controlling the habit, you see.

Sulvie, without looking at me, got up and left the room. A few seconds later I heard water running in the bath.

Zephyr approached, stopping directly in front of me. If you don't leave, she said, her teeth clenched, I'm going to kill you. I swear I will, I am not joking.

I could see she wasn't.

She held the robe collar clenched under her neck. Her eyes were hard and blazing. Her skin was very white, all the make-up scrubbed off. Her hair needed brushing.

Who the hell do you think you are? she asked. We hardly know you. Know nothing about you. We didn't invite you. You practically ruined the party for everyone. You're a truly contemptible human being, do you know that?

I'm sorry you feel that way, I said. As far as the party-crashing goes, you know I came with a friend. My friend assured me you wouldn't mind, that the two of you were very open-minded about that sort of thing.

Yes, she said, her fists balled up at her side, but your friend had the good grace to leave at a proper hour. We didn't have to kick her out. As far as that goes, we hardly know her either.

This surprised me. It had been my impression that Agnes was on the closest of terms with these two women. That was all I had been hearing for months: what an amazing pair this Zephyr and Sulvie were.

She's almost a total stranger, Zephyr went on.

Don't talk to me about Agnes, I said. That woman can drop dead for all I care.

Zephyr was about to say something more when Sulvie appeared, going from the bedroom to the bath, a chocolate-coloured beach towel wrapped around her.

If that man isn't out of here by the time I finish my bath, she said, I am going to kill him.

Zephyr rushed over to her. I could hear them whispering.

Zephyr was asking Sulvie not to leave her alone with me. She was frightened, she said. There was no telling what I might do.

It puzzled me that she should say this. I had not raised my voice to anyone all evening, had not got in anyone's way; since the party ended I had done little more than sit and smoke and say to them over and over not to worry on my behalf, that I'd be leaving soon.

The two women approached together and sat down on the sofa facing me. They stared. For a long time the three of us maintained a strained silence. My ash dropped on the carpet, but I scooped it up so carefully it left no mark. Then Zephyr bounced up, shot at me, and began shaking my shoulders.

What is it you want? she demanded. Is it sex? Do you imagine we will let you sleep with us if you stay long enough?

Sulvie snorted. Fat chance! she said.

You're sick, Zephyr went on, now yelling, slapping at me. You're a cockroach.

He's a bore, Sulvie said.

I wish you wouldn't abuse me like that, I told them. I assure you I mean neither of you any harm. I find you both attractive, to speak frankly, but I certainly have no intention to make advances.

Then what do you want? both shouted at once. Why won't you leave?

I raised my cigarette, nodding at it, by way of impressing on them my firm intention to leave once this last one was smoked down.

Zephyr stopped shaking me. She sucked on a broken nail.

We were all startled when the phone rang. Zephyr snatched it up. She listened a moment, caught Sulvie's eye, then said:

Yes, he's still here. He absolutely refuses to leave.

I moved to take the phone, thinking it was Agnes checking up on me.

Zephyr jumped back. *Don't touch me!* she screamed. Sulvie leapt to her side, both looking panic-stricken. *You leave her alone!* Sulvie hissed.

I sank back down.

No! No! No! Zephyr yelled into the phone. We can handle it! We are quite up to handling this ourselves, thank you! She slammed the receiver down.

The two women returned to the sofa. They sat close together, Zephyr's hand gripping Sulvie's knee, Sulvie with an arm slung around Zephyr's neck.

I was steaming inside my overcoat. My hatband had tightened, giving me a bad headache. I had no more cigarettes.

I had stayed too long simply to get up now and casually walk out. I'd have to exert myself, do my best to win the friendship of these two. I couldn't have them thinking Agnes would waste her time on the contemptible creature they took me to be.

My mouth tasted sour. It seemed to me that if I didn't brush my teeth that very minute I would gag.

May I use your washroom? I asked. That final favour and then I promise you I shall be going.

The women said nothing. They were like lifeless dummies staring back at me.

In their washroom feminine scent abounded. Sulvie's unused bath water had been drawn extremely deep, its steam dampening the blue tiles and mirror. The water was coloured blue. On a white stool beside the tub were folded two thick yellow towels. Their tooth brushes were an identical white. The bristles of the one I chose were hard and cut my gums. I spat out blood, rinsed the toothbrush under a quiet trickle of water, and returned it to its holder.

I looked out. They had not moved from the sofa, although their heads had come together. Their backs were to me; I could not tell whether they were sleeping.

The bathroom was amazingly warm. My face was soaked with sweat. I felt almost too dizzy to stand.

A skylight occupied one entire half of the ceiling. A clever arrangement of shelves extended up to it and on these shelves rested scores of African violets all in bloom and thriving.

Agnes, too, had lately been collecting these dwarfish, uncommunicative plants.

I am a shower person. It has been years since my body has known the luxury of a long hot bath. I slid in, and kept on sliding. The water rose up my chest, my neck, stopping at last just short of my mouth. I sighed back with closed eyes, half-afloat now, very much at peace with myself, wishing only for a book, soft music, or a cigarette.

Shoe Fly Pie

LITTLE MUMMY KEPT ASKING what's wrong, what's wrong, why do you behave like this? Drake doesn't, *I* don't, we're all angels around here except you! You're hardly more than a child, for godsake!

Poor Little Mummy, she stood crying as if someone had poked hot sticks into her eyes.

I didn't say anything, what's the use, if I got balled-up about everything that came along I'd never get anywhere.

Little Mummy said I made her sick, and strode off to look out the picture window at the busy, busy world.

Rain, always rain, what a sopping, dreary neighbourhood.

I wanted to go off and live in a sloop on the China Sea, wouldn't have to put up with crap like this.

The light was streaming through Little Mummy's dress, outlining her legs, strong as a stallion's rear limbs (lots of possibilities there), I thought golly somebody fruity ought to be here to see this, they'd really get a lift out of Little Mummy looking so tough and tall.

Call Drake, I thought, Drake, get your butt in here.

Thump thump thump, her foot was tapping on the hardwood floor, and I knew she was going to say 'I'm going to scream!' even before she said it, and then she did say it, making my skin shiver at my psychic powers.

Nobody can scream like Little Mummy and she knows it.

'Get out of my sight, shithead!' she screeched *before I lose my mind,* which I knew was next.

Christ, the drama, you'd think she'd learned it all from *Days of Our Lives* or *Hospital Story* or such rubbish.

I went on out, things to do.

Not that I felt like it. I had splinters in my bosom, something, fierce aches out front, maybe my boy-friend Jake's left-over hangnails. My nipples festering sore, red craters like those in moon photographs, Jake's eternal gouging.

The slug has been mauling me night after night, saying *give me, give it to me sweetheart, show me the stuff you're made of.*

The crud, why was I so easy?

He doesn't know I've gone off sex, I can hardly be bothered even with *thinking* of it, it's as if I have put on hip-hugger rubber wading boots and drawn them up over my head with a bright Gucci scarf to tie everything off, and it's in these that I splash about. The world as frog pond, just me and Jake gigging for frogs, Little Mummy and the others a million miles off in their own dark ponds with their pitch-forks and flashlights. *Hellooooo over there!*

'Shut up and keep gigging,' says Jake — and, me, I'm easy.

Then in the night when I close my eyes I see ten billion frogs leaping all over the place, while their *croak-croak* mating calls go up like wrap-around fidelics at the Towne's ratfeet cinema.

Time for my annual bird-nesting, I guess, but where's the nest and who has the time?

In my room I flung off my houserobe and stood in front of the mirror. I'm so goddamned pretty. I'm so utterly desirable, so fetching, my tongue hangs out. My patch an adorable thicket, you'd think there would be ram tails and little ram heads sticking out between my legs. Little sheep saying 'Baaa!' And yep, there's Jake's teeth marks on my right breast, his hangnails on my left.

'Real cute, muffin,' he'd say, 'I like to let a lady know when I've dropped in.'

Why doesn't he just open his mouth and swallow me, I thought, the way a nice python snake would?

I had a long, hot, sudsy bath with the candle burning. Nice pine scent. Cheap paperback on the rack, How-To book with everything anybody would ever need to know about how to do oneself in. Reduced sale, buy of the month, at the Classic Bookshop. *Wrist-slashing,* it said, *now this is a popular method, preferred in some instances, though not for everyone. Pill-popping, too, has been given a bad name by the thoughtless over-practice by movie starlets.* No, what the book's author liked best and argued most vehemently for was shoes. *Yes, shoes! Shoes are the classy item, what the what's-with-it people are reaching for this year. Instantly available, comfortable, in a variety of designs! LEGAL! You can go out in style with shoes, and, best yet, with no stigma attached. For the public, God help them, remains totally ignorant of their widespread use as instruments for self-destruction. Look to page 29 for How To.*

What the fuck, I thought, am I supposed to walk myself to death?

I dried off and went head-hanging back to my room. I really wasn't desperate enough to be thinking of these things. Hell, I was only sixteen, had everything to live for. And anything could happen, who knows?

I remembered that story Jake had told me about a man who fell in love with a chicken and used to go into the coop at night and cluck with them, rub the feathers, peck his mouth up against the beak of this fat domino hen. Real upset because he was too heavy, too big, not weighted right to get up on the thin bar and perch, sleep there with them. Maybe tuck his head under the domino's wing.

So what's the fucking *point?* I asked Jake — but that bastard's eyes were snoozing down, said he was flagged out. Getting disgruntled, telling me to shut my mouth, that his beauty-snooze was calling him.

Funny thing was, it was how I felt, in the bed with him, like someone might come in in the morning and start flinging us chicken-feed.

So I got dressed, why not, no need to sit around all day learning How To or listening to Little Mummy snapping at me, asking why I was sitting on my fat behind, *couldn't you at least lift your stupid big feet?*

Poor Little Mummy, truth is I felt some guilt in that quarter. Buckets of gloopy sympathy that one day was going to make my hair fall out. Yet what a lump! I wished she'd made something of her life, maybe gone to night-school, become a professional broadcaster, maybe gone to J. Fitzgerald Business College, taken up home engineering, so she'd at least have learned that the vacuum cleaner, in order to work, must first be plugged *into* a socket. But not Little Mummy. *'It won't work!'* she's always screaming, *'damn thing's broke!'*

Sign of the times, Christ, the inefficiency, the stuff that's *broke* around here, it's enough to make a mule puke. But not me, I've learned How Not To.

I got my hair right, put on my red silk blouse, looked at myself in my red panty hose in the long mirror. I really am a stunner. I certainly am one of the world's most glamorous women. Even an oak fencepost would pull itself up by its roots and run after me. A touch on the cheap side, what the hell, that's spice.

I sat down on the bed and pulled on my boots. Not shiny plastic, thank you, but finest leather, Italian, dyed reddish with tiny black swirls, so soft you'd think you were rubbing up against face powder. But high, up to my crotch. Tad wrinkled in the knees. A good heel. And not a clodhopper's heel either, but one so fabulous in its tooling that it strives with, not against, the styles of all seasons. These boots — they'd cost five hundred dollars if I tried buying them now. But I bought them in the good old days, with baby-sitting money and what change I could find under the sofa cushions after one of Little Mummy's hot dates, back there before that hotshot Drake came along.

(*'That's mine!'* Little Mummy would screech. *'Give me that money, you bitch!'*)

Worn down some, these heels. Way low on the right side, both of them, I guess because that's the way my weight goes.

How I lean. All those right corners I've turned and turned and turned.

Bit thin up in the toe area.

I zipped these boots up, zipper hugging my legs. Real form-fitters.

Beautiful legs, don't know how that rat Jake can ignore them. Not that I give him much chance.

'Take those boots off!' he growls.

I tell him to drop dead.

'No?'

'No.'

But the bastard *knows* something, he doesn't insist.

Guaranteed, these boots are, like the muffler on Jake's car.

The soles are getting thin. I can feel the pavement against my feet, every pebble I walk on, and some days brother is it cold! Snow and slush, well my feet get so frozen some days I feel dizzy, slithers of ice in my head — so dizzy I think maybe I ought to think twice about where I'm going. *What's the rush, kid? Slow down, get a grip on yourself.*

Yeah, *next week,* out in my sloop on the China Sea.

No gigging allowed.

A *huge* rush, I can't help it once I get outside my door, once I catch that scent of the busy, busy world. So much ground to cover and each time thinking *well maybe this time I won't make it, maybe this time the old shoe-fly-pie will hit the fan. It's Boots Up for Rebecca of Sunnybrook Dell.*

But I'm ready now. Bright scarf around the neck and I'm ready again.

'How do I look?' I say to Little Mummy, now busy with her chores.

'Off again? Loo-la-la, aren't *we* the hot ticket today!'

I tell her to take it easy, put the stove on Cook and the house on Hold, try to get a little rest, *House Beautiful* already has its quota of stories for the year.

Little Mummy boo-hoos.

'You're never here when I need you.'

I look closely at Little Mummy. Trying to see if I *can* see, if I look hard enough, something scheming in her. Something more than glaze in her lamppost eyes. Something that says to me *Oh, yes, darling, you ARE my flesh and blood.*

But she is only staring down into the vacuum cleaner pipe. 'Something stuck in there,' she says. She blows into it, concentrating hard. *'I can't see it!'* she cries, and thumps it several times against the kitchen floor. *'That won't help! Nothing helps! How can I fix this thing!'* She rears back, swings it crashing down on the yellow counter top.

Twang twang!

She stands trembling all over, her face stricken, clearly in pain. J. Fitzgerald Business College would have taught her about vibrations. Metal against metal, blood against blood. 'It's *broke!*' she screams. *'Now what the hell do I do? How am I going to clean up this hell hole?'*

Little Mummy, she looks so pathetic in her stocking feet. I feel I could open my mouth and, like a fine witch, devour her.

I plug in the machine.

It roars.

'Oh,' says Little Mummy.

She runs into the living-room and drops down on the sofa, bawling. After a moment she wipes her eyes. She's staring at my boots.

'I always liked those boots,' she sniffles. 'I always wished I had a pair.'

I don't know. I wish I could go to her closet, pull out a pair, my boots or just any old shoes. Bring them to her all buffed up, say, 'Here, baby, put these on.'

And the two of us go out the door side by side, turning right at the corner, setting a good pace, getting out beyond our own and all the old neighbourhoods. Getting out of town, crossing all highways and byways, making a bee-line through wide pasture and up high hill: all the holy unholy world stretching ahead of us and maybe some of it just a little fun, mild bit of pleasure now and again, bit of purpose too if that's not asking too much; and going on, on, always on, higher and faster, getting the scent maybe of good breeze out over the China Sea, sloops leaning against wind — but still going, plopping our feet down *(Hubba-hubba, babe, how you holding up, Little Mummy, how you making it, kid)* — until our shoe-leather finally gives out and we collapse in a heap by the side of the trail.

Hat Pandowdy

HONEYBUNCH WAS DOWN SITTING on the bottom step with her knees spread when I came up the path into the yard. But first thing I saw was the hat. Where are you going with that hat, is what I said. She pretended to be all hummy, not noticing me. 'The sky is churning,' she said, 'be thundering before you know it. Be dark, too.'

I could tell from how she spoke and how she sat — but mostly from her hat — that this was one of her off-days.

I plopped down on the step beside her, my knee next to hers. She was right about the sky and the coming thunder. Honeybunch is right about most things, but she was wrong to be sitting like that. As if she didn't have a care in the world and that, if troubles came, they would pass her right on by. But at the moment I wasn't concerned whether anyone coming up the road would see her. No, the bushes and the weeds would take care of that. I was worried about what her sitting like that, with a hat on and her knees open, was doing to me. It gave me thoughts. It made me wonder about things. But before I could make mention of this, even if I would have, Honeybunch had sprung herself about and thrown both arms around me. 'Let's sit out here and get wet,' is what she said. 'Let's get hip-soaking wet.'

Then she laughed, and I did too, though my heart wasn't in it.

Trouble is, I get thoughts about Honeybunch whether she is laughing or sitting, and no matter how she is sitting. She was always aces with me, and that day I think she knew it.

'Penny for what's making you scowl like that,' she said.

I said I wasn't scowling. That I was just thinking. 'I'm thinking about you,' I said.

She giggled. 'I know that, silly,' she said.

And this time when she flung out her arms they stayed around my neck and pulled me straight over on top of her.

'Can't you tell when I'm in the mood?' she asked.

I said, Yes, I could tell that.

And usually I could, but this time the hat had thrown me. I couldn't figure it out, this hat business.

'Will you shut up about the hat!' she said.

She was in a pique, despite her mood, and it was then that I had my first forewarning. I knew from that moment, from what she said and from how she was fanning her knees and not minding where I looked, that I was headed for trouble.

In the first place, you see, it wasn't her hat, or anyone else's hat I'd ever seen. Also, Honeybunch wasn't the type you'd ever predict would be found dead in one. Hell, she was *opposed* to hats, and far as I know she'd never had one on her head before. So when I came up the path and saw her sitting cool out on the bottom step with this hat on I never would have known it was Honeybunch but for how her legs were spread.

She had nice legs, I'll say that for her.

We went on kissing for a while.

Then it finally got the best of me and I said: That hat, you know, it's really bothering me.

'I don't know why,' she said, 'it's just a hat.'

But her pretended innocence didn't fool me for a minute. I decided it was high time I jumped right in. 'But whose hat is it?' I asked. 'And where did you get it? You're taking a big risk, you know. What are you trying to do to yourself?'

She hunkered down some. I knew she wouldn't like it.

'I only saw one hat like that ever before,' I went on, 'and that was in a picture. Greta Garbo was wearing a hat much like the one you have on, in this picture I saw, and I couldn't think of anything else in the picture until she took her hat off.'

Honeybunch looked at me, a little amazed.

'Of course that was in the old days,' I said. 'She was

playing a spy. In the end she was shot by a firing-squad.'

Honeybunch got huffy.

'Well, I'm not taking this hat off,' she said. 'Nobody's going to shoot me, either.'

'What makes you think you're so different?'

'I'm not so different,' she said. 'You'd be surprised, the number of people around here have the same urges I have.'

That statement really buffaloed me.

We were still kissing. I had my hand up on her thigh, and I pinched her. Not hard, but enough to get her attention.

'Why not?' I said. 'Why won't you take that hat off?'

She gave me one of her Honeybunch smiles. But there was some menace, I thought, behind it. 'This hat's meant to entice,' she said. 'That's what I was told when I bought it and I mean to get my money's worth.'

So that was settled anyway: she had bought it.

Which seemed to me to be about the strangest thing Honeybunch had ever done. So strange I had trouble believing it.

'Just tell me where you bought it,' I said, 'and I'll let the subject drop.'

She said she wouldn't. Couldn't and wouldn't.

We snuggled in for more heavy kissing. She had this scent behind her ears and I kept heading for that.

'I'm enticed anyway,' I told her. 'You don't need that hat.'

Somehow my saying this made her mad. She inhaled a time or two and her backbone hardened. I could tell she was going to get more and more stubborn.

'I need it if I'm wearing it,' she said. 'And I'm wearing it now, so I must need it.'

I took a deep breath, trying to figure all this out. Trying to keep my head clear. Wondering what it is that makes people go off the deep end, as from time to time they do. I could see — and it came as a true surprise to me — that Honeybunch was playing for keeps. She wasn't just joking.

'Anybody don't like this hat can just drop dead,' she said. And she meant it, too.

I took my hand off her bosom and let it drape over my knee. I was getting pretty wrung-out, and pretty disgusted, too. I said, nice as I could: 'Honeybunch, what's come over you? Why are you playing this dangerous game? Maybe you should try explaining yourself.'

'Maybe you should try taking a flying leap,' Honeybunch told me. 'Maybe you should just dry up.'

I didn't argue with her. I don't like spatting with Honeybunch, and anyway I knew we were already long past that. So what I did was move real quick. I made this sneaky-quick movement to snatch the hat off her head and throw it far as I could. But Honeybunch saw what I was up to, and she just held on. I guess she read my eyes and knew what I had in mind. For she held on tight, with both hands, and she wouldn't let go.

'Stop that!' she said. 'You touch this hat and I'll scream! I'll kick you in the nuts if you bother my hat again!'

This did not sound like my Honeybunch of old. I knew I had a real dogfight on my hands. And I wasn't any too sure of victory either. Honeybunch can be tough and fiery when she wants to, and I could see she did. She was all set up to be a real hell-cat.

'Now listen, Honeybunch,' I said. 'Try listening to reason.'

She told me to stuff it.

Funny thing was, I was beginning to get this strange feeling. I was beginning to think that I had known something like this was bound to happen since the first minute I walked up the path and saw Honeybunch out on the step with her legs spread and this hat on. That I had known then that this hat was mean business, that I was headed for nothing but trouble. That my whole life was about to undergo a change.

And that Honeybunch, out on the steps in her hat with her legs spread wide, had known the same. That she was just antsy and headstrong and crazy enough to chance it.

It seemed to me that she'd deliberately set out to mess everything up, to turn our kissing sour and blow everything topsy-turvy.

But I kept silent. Why make matters worse, is what I thought.

'What are you doing?' she asked.

Now that was silly. Any idiot could see what I was doing. And I had sound logic on my side. If we were not going to be kissing any more, if we were going to just sit here talking at cross purposes, then I couldn't see I had any choice.

So I lit one up.

'Go ahead and smoke,' she said after a while. 'You go right ahead and smoke, if you think that's any solution. What do I care?'

So I calmly kept smoking. I smoked it down to the nub. And when that one was finished I lit the next one right off it, and kept on smoking.

Heck, it was my future I was thinking about. It's not every day someone drops a bomb on you like she had.

Honeybunch was real mad now. She had shoved her dress down between her knees and hiked it back up to cover her breasts and shoulders, and she was practically shaking.

'I wouldn't have expected this of you,' she said. 'I expected you'd show a little understanding.'

I told her there were extremes and extremes — and she'd gone right past it.

That truly made her shake.

'If that's how you feel,' she told me, 'you can just turn-tail home! You can get your butt right out of here!'

This little outburst caught me napping. I had a hand down on one of her knees, casually roving.

'Yes, you can scat!' she said. 'You can motor right on out of here.'

No, I hadn't expected any sudden moves on her part, not of that order. I had been watching the sky tumbling and bubbling off on the horizon, and half-way thinking about that, wondering how soon it would get dark and when the rain would come and whether I should do any more with that knee of hers. Maybe get those knees apart again, the way they'd been when I found her. There was this black and red and yellow butterfly — what they call a Lepidoptera Some-thing-or-Other — flitting about over the weeds, fluttering along all zigzaggy, in no particular direction, the way they do, and down on this wild daisy patch were two or three of those smallish white butterflies, sipping the juice of daisy or whatever it is they do, with their little wings more or less preening, the wings up tight together like what they most wanted to do was hug themselves. Down near the road in this smooth level spot the wind was twisting up in a funnel a fine swirl of dust, and what I was half-thinking, my mind attuned to nature as it was, and only idly stroking Honey-bunch's knee, was something of this order: Well, by God, there it is, ESSENCE OF FEMALE, right here in front of me. For it had struck me that what Honeybunch had in mind with this hat business wasn't so different from what I was seeing out there in nature. But then before I could get my brains sorted out the whole idea sort of scooted away and only this blank spot was left where the idea had been, and I thought, Yep, that's what this female business does to a man, it just leaves him shaking his head, hardly knowing up from down or sideways from flat. So all I could do was throw up my hands and give a sick, disgusting look at Honeybunch in her hat, which was what had set my brains in motion in the first place. ESSENCE OF STUPIDITY, is what I thought then, for that's where it always got you in the end — got you thinking, Well, heck, I must be crazy for thinking one can draw paral-lels between *hats* and *butterflies*, I must be out of my flipping mind. Pretty soon, I thought, I'd be acting as batty as Honey-bunch herself.

So that's the kind of stuff I was turning over when Honey-bunch came up with this 'Scat!' business, with her face turning blue and her breath coming hard, now standing up and shaking her fists in my face and telling me what I could do with myself.

'You can get your butt off my property,' she said, 'that's what you can do!'

Oh boy, she was really hot.

'Butt out!' she said. 'Beat it!'

And a second later she had tromped across the porch, dived inside, and locked and bolted the door behind her.

Well, I'd always known she was impulsive.

'We're through!' she hollered. 'I'd sooner die than put up with the likes of you! So shove off! Just go like a bat out of hell!'

Now that pained me. It put a big hard ache dead under my skin. Before tonight Honeybunch and me had been making plans. We'd figured out who would sit where and where the icebox would go and who would look after the accounts. We'd mapped out a pretty good future for ourselves.

'Buzz off!' Honeybunch cried. 'Get lost!'

I thought of arguing with her. Thought of saying something sweet that might soften her mood. Work on her sympathies. Remind her of what we meant to each other. But I didn't have it in me. I was interested, and wanted to, but I'd lost the juice.

Fatalism, I guess that's what it was.

And I was partly in a daze. This whole hat business had me spinning. What do you know, I said to myself. Imagine Honeybunch acting this way! You never would have guessed it! Maybe you're best to be out of it! Maybe what she's shown tonight is her true self!

But I was by no means sure. Old Honeybunch and me, we'd had us some good times. And I knew I'd be a long time finding another woman with her special gifts. With her magic and flair.

So I moped. It was like a part of me had dropped right down through the floor.

'Ar you sure, Honeybunch?' I asked. 'Your mind's made up?'

But she didn't answer. There wasn't a sound inside.

'Well, I'm going,' I said. 'This is it, I guess.'

Not a whisper. I tried peeking through the window, but nothing was doing.

I had a hunch Honeybunch might have zipped out out the

back door, that I'd find her now out there cutting across the field. So I went flying around back. But my hunch proved wrong. Some chickens were clucking about, trying to get in a few last pecks before their bedtime, but that was about all. Two or three of them were already up in the trees, head under wing. One sorry hen came up and pecked a number of times at my boot.

That was chickens for you. Not a brain between them.

I took a look through a crack in the back door. And there was Honeybunch sitting in this old rocker, looking pretty as you please, with her knees up and a glass of something in her hand. Tea, it looked like. And flipping through a magazine. Smiling, even. Looking as contented as could be, with this big hat flopping down over her face.

Jesus God. It truly astonished me. Not an ounce of remorse anywhere on her.

Now that, I thought, really takes the cake.

I was so stunned I couldn't even speak.

What I did was I came around to the front and sat a few minutes out on the step, smoking and humming. Talking to myself. You've learned a lot *today*, I told myself. It will be a far cry in December before you forget *this*!

I watched it get dark. I saw the sky bubbling and boiling, lightning flashing, the tree-tops swaying. Saw the rain coming.

It would all have been pretty, any other day.

Finally I picked myself up and ambled on down the path. It was all overgrown and ugly and I couldn't see why Honeybunch hadn't at least tried to cut down some of the taller weeds. Get rid of these briars. It seemed to me a person ought to take some pride in where and how she lived.

Funny thing, I had never thought of Honeybunch as lazy.

Two or three of her dogs started barking. I told them to hush up. But they didn't so I flung a few sticks their way. A few stones, too. One of them yelped. I guess I hit it. It was too dark now to see. The others kept on yowling.

It put my back up, hearing those mongrels going on like that. What I ought to do, I told myself, is get me some poison. That would shut them up. It was beginning to make some sense to me, this business of the hats. I could see how it saved a person from a lot of mistakes. How it kept him from hooking up with the wrong party.

Spread knees and fine legs and a fiery disposition, that was one thing. But this hat trick of hers, that's where her real metal shone through.

One of the dogs now was howling. Low and rubbing, a real wolf call. It gave my skin the goose bumps. Now if it was me, I said, I'd definitely get rid of them. I'd want the peace and quiet. But Honeybunch goes her own way. We'd had us a lot of talks about those dogs.

What I might do, I thought, was come back one night, lay out a few bear traps.

Out where the path met the lane I stopped and looked back. The house was dark, not a lamp at any window. Well, if she's smart, I thought, she'll keep it that way. It truly was black and gloomy, as sorry a place as any I'd ever seen. It baffled me how I'd ever stumbled onto such a miserable, shut-up looking house in the first place. It was damn near rotted and half-tumbled over and one strong kick would have finished it off.

No, I thought, I should have known when I first come to this place what my coming was all going to come down to in the end.

I should have had better sense.

But she'd been sitting out on the steps that time too, with her knees open, washing her hair. So thick and long she could hardly keep it out of the bucket.

Real pretty sight. She'd really made my heart turn over.

'Hand me that towel,' she'd said.

Dress bunched up in her lap, with not a thought to covering herself. Nor minding that her front was open to the world.

'You got nice hair,' I'd said.

'You're crazy,' she'd said, 'if that's where you're looking first.'

I should have known then I had me a koo-koo.

Now what I hated most, staring back at it, was what she'd done to the place to try and make it pretty. A place a couple could share.

'You and me could live here,' she'd said. 'We could take out those stumps and clear off a level space out back. Put in corn.'

Pie in the sky, that's all that had been.

I went on down the lane. Thanking God I'd found out her true colours in time.

The dogs' barking and howling finally got distant, and finally not there at all. What I mean is, you had to stop and strain your ear to hear them. The wind was sweeping up fast now, the air getting moist, and you could see — well, I could — the white boney flash of lightning . . . and a second or two later, the clapping thunder. It put me in mind of two giant wash-tubs clanging, how it rumbled on.

I walked the lane from memory, unable to see, and not much caring. I was in no hurry to get where I had to be going. Let her have an hour or two of peace, I thought, I owe her that much.

But she had it coming, that's how I felt. She deserved it. And pretty soon she'd be singing a different tune.

For I couldn't get it out of my mind, her sitting there in the rocker, sipping on tea, looking pleased as peaches with herself.

Then something odd happened. Down in the hollow, where it was black as a pit and where at night I'd always felt uneasy, I heard this beat of horse hooves behind me, the clatter of wagon wheels, and I pressed back against the bushes to let the thing pass. Some fool racing along in the dark, is what I thought. Be lucky he don't kill himself.

But I already had this prickle down my backside. Maybe some sweat on my brow as well, for it is always down in the hollow that this kind of business happens to me. The clatter grew louder, the hooves came faster, I heard this whip snapping, heard the horse's heavy breathing — felt this sudden swoosh of wind on my face. SWOOSH! — and I'm leaning back, feeling it streak by, not an inch from my buttons . . . then the sound is gone, just petering out. And me left wondering. For I never saw a thing. Not a blessed glint or gleam. Nothing at all. And this was strange, for although it was *getting* to be black as pitch it wasn't *yet* pitch, and I should have seen it. Should have, had it been there.

A moment later the rain whirled down. It dropped that way, in a whirl, heavy as buckets. In a matter of seconds I was soaked to the skin. It poured on me and around me and my boots went *swug-swug*. But I didn't mind. It felt nice, being cooled off, and coming at last up out of the hollow.

So I went on at my regular pace.

Where the road turned I went straight, directly on up the mountain, up a narrow trail that I and others follow sometimes for the short cut. The weeds were pretty high, it was steep and rocky. I caught a few limbs in the face. Slipped a couple of times. Lost my boot once, and had to go rooting around in mud to find it. But the climbing was easy for me, all in all. I'm fit, and knew what I was doing.

One time one of the limbs smacked me real hard and I caught at it and twisted on it, and pulled, trying to yank it away from its trunk, and what was funny about this was what I kept saying. 'Choke Honeybunch,' is what it was. 'Just choke her!'

For I'd got to thinking that Honeybunch had done me a deep wrong, that she'd truly thrown a wrench into our plans. It seemed to me that what she'd done was rotten as dirt, and not just rotten but pretty near the root of all evil. 'So choke her!' I said — and I kept on twisting and yanking, but the limb wouldn't give.

Temper is what that was. And it amazed me a little.

It was not long after this that I crossed over the ridge, up past this tight stand of trees, and got my surprise. That I

111

crossed over and found I had company. In front of me I saw this unhitched wagon, with something beneath it, and this fine tall horse tied up to a bush. It looked like a horse anyway, and was stomping about like one, but I made most of this out from the occasional flash of lightning and by straining until my eyes popped. Except for the lightning, I could hardly see my hands in front of me. So I went up closer, taking things easy. Going slow, because it wasn't my aim to walk blind into a place where I wasn't wanted or needed.

Puddles were all about and rain-water kept pouring over my eyes.

What I couldn't figure was how the horse and wagon had got up the mountain. It didn't make any sense. Anybody with two wits about them wouldn't even have tried.

'Who's there?' I called. 'What's up? What's going on here?'

I heard this furry sweet voice that seemed to be coming from under the wagon. Some woman's voice. Furry and strange and pretty much on the eerie side.

'What's that?' I asked. 'Who are you?'

There it came again, just as sweet, but a bit more insistent.

I stepped in closer. And then the sky lit up and I saw her, crouched under the wagon, more or less sitting on her heels, beckoning to me.

'Young man. Young man,' she kept saying. *'Come here.'*

A black lump, that's all she was. Or, anyway, I saw no face. Just lumpy folds of cloth. Eerie, I say. Enough to make my skin crawl.

'Young man. Young man. Come here.'

Yep, that's what she was saying all right.

Well, I'm not that young, and I'm hardly the kind that leaps as instructed, but pretty soon I was crouched down myself, holding onto the rear wheel, looking in at her under the wagon.

'Closer,' she said. *'Come closer.'*

She had a very dark face. In fact, she was dark all over.

Not that I could see her that clearly. But for the rustle of her garments I'd have hardly known where to look.

'*Closer,*' she said. '*Come here.*'

I dropped to one knee and ankled my way directly up to her. It was then that I saw the hat. It was not the same hat Honeybunch had been wearing, but nevertheless it was a hat. The brim sort of curved and she had it swooped down over one ear.

I decided I'd best not dwell on it. That the least I could do was be civil.

'Why are you crouched under this wagon?' I asked.

'Why?' Her voice went way up. You'd think I had said something half-crazy. 'Why? To keep my hat from getting wet, of course!'

This struck me as a thing so outrageously silly that it was all I could do to keep from laughing. From that, or throttling her.

But I saw she was shivering.

'Oh, I'm cold,' she moaned. 'I'm so cold I can't think straight. Nobody told me it was so cold up here.'

'It's cold,' I said, 'I'll grant you that.'

Next thing I knew she had her hand in mine. She was tugging me towards her. 'So cold,' she said. 'Why don't you put your arms around me? I hate being cold.'

'Everyone does,' I said.

And I meant to have nothing to do with her — in the first place because I didn't know her and in the second place because I didn't much like her — but she was trembling so violently, and making such cold, snatchy noises, that I too began to feel cold.

So I put my arms around her.

This gave me quite a shock, for in fact she was instantly warm, and instantly pressing herself against me. Snuggling in close as she could.

'You're warm now,' I said. 'Christ, you're practically on fire.'

She laughed in a funny, satisfied, genuinely wicked way. That's how it sounded to me. And I wondered, as I heard it, whether I wasn't headed into trouble. But I got no time to think about this, because she was kissing my neck and kissing my ears and my face and everywhere else she could find bare skin.

'You smell so lovely,' she said in a whisper. 'So wet and warm and lovely I could eat you up.' And her hands started running under my clothes and over my legs, and all the time she kept snuggling and pressing and kissing.

'Caress me!' she sighed. 'Really caress me!'

Funny thing, too, because that's exactly what I was doing.

'Let's stretch out,' she said. 'It's so smooth and dark and nice under here.'

Well, we already were stretched out. I was right down on her, about as intertwined with her as two bodies could be. And my eyes were closed too, and we were both moaning, and it seemed to me I felt about as good and nice as I ever had. But I was glad she wasn't Honeybunch because it struck me that there was something a bit cheap about it. Bit on the tacky side, I mean.

I wasn't so sure I respected her. I wasn't sure I knew what I was doing.

All the same, I was certainly enjoying it.

I had become convinced that, whatever else she might be, she was certainly very beautiful. She *felt* beautiful. In fact I was astounded and could hardly believe how beautiful she did feel.

Even so, things were not right.

'Take your hat off,' I said.

It's possible she didn't hear me. It was stormy, lightning was flashing, and the horse was getting restless, hoofing about. Rain, too, was splatting down, and wind gushing about.

'No,' she said, 'take anything, but not my hat!'

To cap matters off, she laughed, and went on squirming and kissing and hugging.

Me, too, though much of my spark had died.

'One more chance,' I said. 'Take it off.'

She again said no.

I began to think she and Honeybunch were in collusion. Maybe, even, that they had planned this between them.

I didn't like it.

It seemed to me that something was rotten in the state of Denmark.

I snatched at the hat, and pulled. I kept pulling and the hat wouldn't come loose and finally I brought my shoes up against her body and pushed hard as I could, pushed as I pulled, but the hat didn't budge.

'Why must you wear it?' I asked, utterly vexed. 'What possible importance can it have?'

Her kisses got hotter.

But I kept pulling. I couldn't see how I was pulling and kissing at the same time, but that's precisely what I was doing. I had to have the hat off, no way around it.

'You can't have it,' she wept. 'I can't let you.'

It was obvious, despite her kisses and her moaning and her spider-limbed body wrapped around mine, what came first. Hats did. Wet kisses didn't hold a candle to them.

'Off!' I screamed. 'Take it off!'

'Never!' came her screech back. 'Not my hat! Anything, any time, but not my hat!'

'Now!' I said. 'This minute! I'm giving you your last chance!'

'Oh don't deny me my essence!' she wailed. 'Don't deny me what it is that makes you want me in the first place!'

I was plain worn out with malarky of this kind. It was time I got rough. I gave her a whopping big kick in the head.

'You can't have it!' she moaned. 'I'd rather die!'

It struck me that this was a most extreme remark for her to make. Most bizarre. It showed she'd totally gone round the bend.

Christ, you'd think these hats were made of gold, that their very souls were dependent on them. It seemed to me that she and Honeybunch and all of the others were being absolutely vixenish and tawdry to wag on about these hats, that they were being low-down and contemptible and thoroughly inexcusable.

Give an inch, I thought, and they take a mile.

You wouldn't find *me* acting that way, is what I thought.

'*Off!*' I said. '*Now! Or take your medicine!*'

'*No!*' she said, just as enthusiastically.

So I did what I had to do. Did what they'd been driving me to do all along. Did it, and don't regret it.

Of course it was ugly. It was downright horrible, and made my blood curdle. But I did it.

And I'm not saying it was right — just that it was necessary. For that's the rule out here. No Hats. Like it or leave it. *No Hats!* And that's the final word.

Order has to begin some place.

I mean, there's the common good to think about.

The horse had the jitters. I went over and rubbed her down for a bit, giving her a soft talk in the ear.

'There, there, little lady,' I said. 'Calm down. It's all over now.'

Then I went back under the wagon, out of the storm. Hard chunks were falling, hail I guess.

I was bruised all over.

Once daylight came I hitched up the horse and slung her body up on the wagon, and brought her on in. The officials didn't like it — they never do — but they had no choice but to accept the load and get on with the dirty work.

'Another hat case, huh?' one of them said.

I said yeah.

A guy wearing a Sam Browne belt came out and poked at her hair with a stick. 'Too bad,' he said. 'But she was asking for it all right.'

We stared a moment at her shoes. They were pretty fancy, too. But about borderline, we figured.

'Wonder what comes over them?' someone else said. 'What gets *into* them? I can't understand it.'

We all shook our heads. What the heck. We all knew it was a mystery we'd never get to the bottom of. We'd given up trying.

'Honeybunch, too, eh?' he went on. 'Now I never would have predicted her.' He sighed a bit. 'Well, I guess we'd best go and get her.'

And there they went, out after her.

Poor Honeybunch, I thought.

She'd had a good chance at life but had to go wreck it.

Hats. I wished they'd never been invented.

The rain had slackened some and you could make out a clear patch in the sky, down there at one end, above the steeple.

'Storm's passing,' I said.

'I hope to God so,' somebody answered.

I was signing a few last forms and getting set to get out of there, when a small contingent of troops came in. They looked tired and beat-down and smelled of smoke.

I asked one of them what was up.

'Big raid,' I was told. 'Over at the General Store.'

'You get much?' I asked.

'Cases,' he said. 'Cases and cases. I'm going to have nightmares for the rest of my life.'

Me too, I thought.

'Well, hell,' I said, shrugging it off, 'be something to tell the kids, I guess.'

Everybody nodded. We all lit up.

Outside, the fire was going strong up at the General Store. The flames were really licking. It was all black and smokey, the smoke just tumbling over. Now and then someone would run up and pitch something in it. A bunch of lookers-on was up on the sidewalk, behind ropes. A number of women were lying out on the street, kicking and screaming, trying to get loose. They surprised me, a few of them, for they were people I recognized, some pretty high-up in the town. A little girl, maybe four years old, went running by, wearing what some people might call a hat, though I'd say it was more like a paper bag with bird feathers stuck to it. A woman in a big oil slicker was chasing her, the mother I guess, screeching out her name, as panicky as could be. She caught her by the legs and threw her down and snatched off the bag hat and slapped the little idiot's face a time or two. Then she ran up weeping and pitched the feathered thing into the blaze.

I could see the officials trying to decide which way to go on it, but finally they turned their backs, deciding they hadn't seen it.

Well, that was law and order for you. I'd know who to vote for next time.

The little kid zipped off. Bawling.

It was the younger people really getting into the thick of things. They were snatching scarves and jewelry, even the odd purse — from any woman crazy enough to be wearing them — and throwing those in.

One woman in high heels got herself singed.

The guy from the beauty parlour was out in front of his place, looking sick. I don't know why — he hadn't been getting much trade anyhow.

I kicked stones, heading over to the picture place. Feeling pretty dejected. They'd be getting out to Honeybunch's place pretty soon. I hoped she'd had sense enough to run, but I doubted it. The flames were leaping truly high now over the General Store. The smoke was awful chokey. If they didn't watch it the fire was going to spread and catch some other places. Maybe burn up the whole darned town.

The flashing light bulbs at the picture place looked kind of pathetic, compared to the fire. But I crossed on over. I didn't even bother to check the marquee, just plunked down my money, and walked in. The picture was already playing and I pretty much had my choice of seats. It was another old one, Deanna Durbin, I think. Somebody like that.

It was hard following sometimes, because of the cuts. But it had a good story. And the music was good.

Hitting the Charts

LAST NIGHT I WAS out doing the boogie.

Nothing at The Ruptured Duck, not much at Teen Town or The Gypsy Moth, but at The Hot Wire I read the vibes, contemplated my juices, and determined I was all set to get lucky.

My hour had been a long time coming.

It was a case of *Go Daddy Go*, of *macho macho* and *Disco Duck*, or give your heart to Old Mother Nature and *let the cool lady sink you on down.*

> *I got no money*
> *and I got no friend,*
> *Me by my lonely*
> *and nearing the end.*
> *I got no wife*
> *and I got no love,*
> *Me by my lonely*
> *Living push and shove.*

I located a lovely person, foxy # with drooping head, sitting alone at a table in a far corner the minute my eyelids cooled. This is the life, Dad, I told myself — and putting on my Ready For Anything face I hiked up my Truckstop Designer jeans and motored over.

'Dance with me Henry,' I cried, and gave her The Look.

Without giving me a glance or saying a word she hoisted herself up and like a stately breeze headed out to the floor. I followed fast behind, chasing the scent of Wind Song by Prince Matchabelli, as the music wheeled into high screech like a thousand jibjabs finally let out into the garden.

Ta-ta-tum ta-ta-tum, let the beat go on. I gave my hips their first twist and was off and running like a nag bolting the gate, throwing out my arms in a propeller spin so that no one could doubt which part of the floor was mine.

'I'm Jake,' I told my partner on the up-breath, 'how you making out?'

Nothing. Under her bangs her moon face looked like an opening cut out of deep hedge. Never mind. I went up on first one toe and then the other, bending like green timber. In my high school days Jake B. Carlyle had been known as the eagle of the dance floor and it was all coming back after 99 years.

Wang Wang Blues, I thought, *and Begin the Beguine, gonna take a sentimental journey.*

'You come here often?' I shouted.

No reply. Her sight was always on someone just behind me, never any movement up or down. Her noble head slid from shoulder to shoulder like a thing on rails.

'That's pretty groovy,' I joked, 'you pick that up in India?'

Not a flicker. Yet her very essence told me I was getting somewhere.

Butter in my hands, *yeah-yeah-yeah!*

I had come a long way in only a few hours. At the start of the evening the music had been like a rhino herd having a singalong with Mitch; I had left The Ruptured Duck and Teen Town a Hippo on skate boards, but now I was hitting my stride. Jake, I told myself, your azimuth is in its five moons, Jupiter is high, and the time is yours! I had come through four repeat years at the Transcendental Meditation Centre, gone fourteen months with the Technocracy crowd, for twenty-seven years had been a devout Rosicrucian, and for one season had been a scrub guard for the House of David. Had spent half a lifetime kicking pigeons or just generally floundering about, but now my head was in place.

Daddy don't step on my Dr. Scholl's shoes because my clock has turned and the hour is ripe! I have weathered Frankie Laine's Jezebel and Spike Jones' Beatlebomb and my ears no longer extended to my feet. I was Fritz the Cat and purring out loud over all of discoland *Oh Mama we are the most, we are hot-to-trot tonight, your feet are on fire and Bo Diddly I aint.*

The platter ripped to its demise. Strobe lights blinked and for an instant they let the tape deck cool. 'Buy you a drink?' I said, and fifty arms shot up — though my own sweet dancing partner was nowhere to be seen.

I was bathed in black mud, a sightless knave. *Frail,* I thought, *oh frail is thy hand in mine, my fair Caithleeene!*

'Open the door Richard,' I cried, 'oh Richard open that door!'

Never mind. I was at home with these hard-to-get types and felt confident that before the evening ended I'd have her licking from my hands. Already I loved her air of indifferent and placid mystery, her aura of divine and mystic depth; I loved the way her hair bounced above expressionless ears and how her chin never dropped and how the light wheel grazed like sheep on her face. She was mine all mine and just the kind of sweet perfection I was looking for. *Mama Mama Mama*, I cried to the rafters, *treat me good!*

The platter spun anew and I quivered in my tracks, going solo for a while. Two or three of those I bumped gave me dirty looks and one in a feather-duster skirt and a strontium 90 smile murmured in my ear, 'You better slow down, Pops, your face is snow-white, you definitely got lily-pad gills.'

'I'm cooking with gas,' I told this smiler, 'no need to worry,' and gave her a toad-footed spin that had her eyes rattling in her head.

Oh Jelly Roll roll, cream me no cream and butter me no butter.

I was beginning to get the feel of my digs. Beginning to realize what I had been missing out on by not doing the boogie scene long before. Beginning to regret all my tortured years of Monday Nite Baseball and Friday Nite poker and Saturday Nite blues and the thousand bleak evenings sitting on my elbows.

Jake, I told myself, this is the high life, the real life, this is where it's at, old fossil-heart of mine, you're to turn over a new leaf dating from now.

No more four A.M. movies for me, with the final blip dropping like man's last breath across the snowballed screen. No more weeping in the solitude of all my betrayals and longing for dawn's tender mercy to tuck me up in my drunken bed.

Oh frail is thy hand in mine, oh frail is your touch, my darling Caithleene.

I was clearly cut out for this fine night-life. It was *Groovy Greybeard Groovy* and proper time I took off my age-old bib.

I grabbed a spin with loose flotsam whose date was spewing up Labatt's 50 in a corner, and kept her there for a full ten minutes while the Gyroscopes wooed us with power-pack song and the smoke of cigarettes dropped from the black ceiling inch by inch and wrote death in the air with a thousand white signatures, and when finally she wiped off the sweat and said 'Um tarred' I took my cues and hurried her back to her tongue-tied mate, murmuring *merci* and *toute la guerre* as a gentleman would, in the meantime keeping a wary eye out for my Dream Girl, the one fair lady in the whole of The Hot Wire whom I would woo and be wooed by and whom I would have.

But man is an island even at The Hot Wire and my Dream Girl was nowhere to be seen and it was all Lover's Lullaby for me.

I'll love her in the attic,
I'll love her in the cellar
I'll love her wherever
She's clearly ecstatic.

Oh frail your hand, Caithleeene. Oh your time was long time a-coming, Willie Mays.

I elbowed my way up to black marble bar and told the cherub behind it to splash down in front of me whatever poison was nearest to hand, hang the expense, my son.

Set'um up Joe.

A man in a trench coat wide as a flag gave me a hearty slap on the shoulder and asked if I was from out of town, foot-loose and fancy-free the same as him. 'Portland myself,' he shouted, 'USofA, city county and nation built by God.' But now and then, he confessed, he had to unwind. He fished out a card and waved it in front of me: CHARTERED ACCOUNTANTS, it read, FITZ, DIBBS AND SLIDE — *We Have What Counts* . . . . 'Dibbs,' he said, throwing out a hand, 'put'er there.' He laughed, the joker, and went into a quick crouch, all better to goose a young lady just then passing by. The lady shrieked and spun, though not before Dibbs was again upright and innocently staring off into the dim yonder. The lady stared at my outstretched hand which Dibbs had refused, then reared back and smacked her mighty fist against my face.

'Reprobate,' she snarled, and scooted on.

Oh Daddy shoot me with novocaine! Oh Mama, tell me the news!

'Works every time,' snickered Dibbs. 'I pulled that trick on Fitz one time and he lost three teeth.' He grabbed at my arm, pulled me along: 'Let's go visit the Men's. In this sumphole I can't hear myself think.'

I was grateful, once reaching the Men's, for my Life by Riley platform heels. They let me tower over Dibbs, shorter than a barber pole and about as cool, and moreover kept my flared cuffs dry.

'Portland's all right,' ventured Dibbs, looking for a high spot to perch, 'but there are things a man can't do in his own home town. Too many twinkies he has to look out for. In Portland, city of God, you wouldn't find me coming within a mile of a dump like this.'

'Time waits for no man,' I told this snake. 'Shake, rattle, and roll.' Scratches in the door behind which Dibbs hid himself told me to CALL GLORIA, first with the latest, last with the most. Stickers on the wall said NO NUKES and SAVE OUR

SEALS and REMEMBER PEARL HARBOR and GOD ADORES A
TURKEY.

'A man's got to break out of a rut,' Dibbs was telling me.
'Got to get his arms around something unfamiliar now and
then. You got a paper I could read? Mind you,' he said, 'the
wife don't understand, but I say what the hell, a quick poke
never hurt anyone. These young people now, not worth a
crap, but they have the right idea. I tell you it's places like
this that's keeping old Dibbs feeling young.'

I sloshed down my gin, hardly listening to Dibbs, floating
back to the action on wings of song, thinking how I had
found and lost my thrill on Blueberry Hill, on Mood Indigo
and Rock Island Line. Sock it to me, baby, I told old Dibbs,
these shoes were made for walking, now who's got the
smack?

'My daughter, 17,' Dibbs went on, 'precious lamb, she's
hot-to-trot for experience, can't wait to run off with the first
dog-catcher sniffs up her skirt. Last week I caught her
writing Ann Landers, complaining how her parents kept her
penned up, "they don't trust me," she said. Oh I lit into her, I
really told her where she stood. I smelt smoke the other day
walking into her room, and my fist nearly took off her head.
She'll think twice next time. She sees me taking a drink at
home, asks "why can't I have one?" I tell you I've got blisters
from the times I've had to smack that child. My daddy
smacked me around, what do you think, that I'd disapprove?
How else you imagine I got where I am? Not long ago I came
home, found some squirt kid trying to sneak away through
the backyard. I pulled him back inside, punched his nose,
kicked him in my den. My den is redwood panelled, most
beautiful stuff you ever saw. I got 14 rifles mounted, collec-
tor's items, every one in working order. Blow the head off a
moose, great weapons, I tell you a person don't even have to
aim. I said, "there they are, kid, take your pick." "Whut,
huh?" he said — I tell you kids today don't even know
human speech. "You got it, kid," I told this squirt, "the next

time you come nosing round my daughter you going to get my .12 ought right between your eyes." Oh that kid scrammed, I tell you we're raising nothing but chickens these days. In my day I'm proud to say I was mauling cherries all over town, me and jailbait had a natural attraction for each other. You think I don't know what is going on? What kids have in mind? Now the Kooks you find in here, these laid-back dope fiends living off my tax — if I found my daughter sleeping around like these Kooks I'd choke her, no questions asked. She knows it too. Oh she hoes the line. A sweet girl, a precious angel. You should have seen that letter she was writing Ann, just as proper as you please. Me, I'd spend a week on it and still not have the commas right. That's education, that's what I'm paying for. I mean, a parent's got to contribute, right? Out here, out in the real world, well it's all going to hell in a handbasket quicker than the eye can blink, wouldn't you say? But I've got faith, I'm a bundle of love, none of that negative crap for me.'

Groovy, I thought, *Oh Daddio, show me the way.*

'Oh boy!' Dibbs said, jacking up his pants, 'that felt good, third time I been today, healthy sign, wouldn't you say?' — and without a sprinkle of water over his hands but with time to slick back his receding hair he was off and running, leaping back into the fray. 'I can still git it up,' he shouted back, 'don't think I can't.' He crowded a friendly neighbour off a bar stool and scrambled up huffing, his brow shining with sweat, while a multitude of white gulls dipped their wings in a slow circle overhead, part of the decor that gave The Hot Wire its classy name. The beat was whining out of a half-dozen ceiling vents with a kamikaze craze and the floor was pounding and at the tables a hundred good-time voices were screeching in gratitude. It was meal time at the Oasis and I was with it, baby, I was Johnny on the Spot, old Johnnie B. Kool.

'Long may your willy ream,' shouted Dibbs, now off to the dance floor, grabbing at every feline shape, 'I've got more notches than Billy the Kid and I mean to dip it while the dippin's good.'

Oh Mama, I thought, *Oh hunter home from the hill, Oh man in the Grey Flannel Suit. Oh make me a pallet on the floor. Oh it ain't me, babe!* Gyrating couples shook past under waves of yellow, mauve and blue. I yearned to step forward and embrace each of them, to say *Oh you spinning swingers, what you see here is a man who takes his lessons from Father Time, from the Mole People who burrow every year in my yard. September Song and Autumn Leaves and Some Enchanted Evening, all that is smoke in my eyes. Shoot Tchaikovsky, give the mickey to Mahler, old B. is bleeding on the floor. I emerge each year new-born and ripe for action. I have shucked Paul Harvey's Decade of News, I'm Johnny Belinda On-the-Spot. Butter me no butter and Yule me no Yule, I want all your wooden nickels, old Dibbs and I will talk them into gold.*

Hubba-hubba, babe, wake up little Suzy, take me to the hop!

Oh frail is they hand in mine, how frail,
my fair Caithleeene.

A man with an undertaker's face, seated by the woman next on his list, leaned into my shoulder, said, 'I'm from Saskatoon, that's my wife Munchie I'm with. Say hello to the nice man, Munchie.' Munchie glowered, then showed her red tongue, pulling at my sleeve. 'What a character,' she said. 'I was wed once and that was enough.' I sank down beside this wind-swept pair, yearning for Saskatoon where I've never been, for the Mom and Pop I'd have there waiting for me to make something of my life. No doubt the woman I should have married was still waiting for me, waiting in Saskatoon. Her life had been ruined, mine too, because I hadn't had the good sense to stay where I was born and with what was good for me, this dream-time Saskatoon. She would have lived next door, would have initiated me gently into sex, would have urged me to put my life back together and not commit suicide after losing the race for high school presidency by 900 votes. *You can do it, Jake, I've always believed in you. Oh Jake, there's always next year. Oh Jake, you did this when they dropped you from the checkers team.* Happy kids, a sound business of my own, all waiting in Saskatoon. Big warm house, couple of cars, a good snowblower to keep our driveways clear.

I could have made it big in Saskatoon.

'Look at him,' the undertaker man said. 'Saskatoon's got him. Happens every time.'

'Buy me some peanuts,' his Munchie said, 'how do you like my hair?'

Adios, Saskatoon.

When I hear you call ... my love song ... to me. ...

I went in search of my dream girl. I tapped the wrong beauty on the shoulder and the boy-friend rose up from his chair to stand on my toes. The music was loud and I didn't take in the advice he was giving, though his beauty's voice left no room for any misunderstanding: '*Go suck eggs,*' she said. '*Cock your leg up to a fire hydrant, buzz off, me and him are here to have us fun.*' Under these scrofulous urgings, I chug-lugged on.

Oh broken-hearted melody, oh melancholy baby, I'm coming round the mountain yes I am.

The floor was solid concrete but I could feel it vibrating. Before the place became The Hot Wire it had been Elmo's Body & Fender Shop. Under this very ceiling where gulls circled and lights flashed 3000 times to the single blink Elmo's drab crew had put on a new grill and bumper, new radiator, new hood and paint job after my erstwhile wife, unable to give up sweets and tormented by broken fingernails, had tried to drive her Volkswagen through our very own front door. Lovely woman, she'd sat on the red seat screeching out through broken glass that there '*was not power enough under the hood!*' Then to back up and come again, knowing I was in there somewhere.

I'm all for you, body and soul.

Where was old Elmo now, I wondered. And erstwhile

wife, where was she? They too ought to be here doing the boogie, didn't know what they were missing.

Dibbs punched me on the arm, shoved me back against a wall.

'Got change?' he demanded. 'Any change?'

'Oh yeah, yeah,' I said, and commenced digging.

'A dollar? Two dollars? My old lady don't take collect calls any more not since our oldest went Yo-yo and cut out on us. Calls all the time, wants to speak to God. A fruit-cake, can you imagine, my son!'

He scratched at my palm, took what change I had.

'Got to report in, you know,' he explained, going. 'Conference, you know! Midnight oil, what Dibbs won't do to keep together house and home!' He smacked his brow, came back at me again. 'How you fixed? Anything to spare? A loan? Woman over there with the navel cut, skinny as a playing card, I asked her how much, she gave me the wink. Let you have seconds, what do you say?'

I plonked down a dollar into his hand. Added another.

'Go for quality tonight,' I told him, 'it's all on me.'

Ah, your hand in mine, Caithleeene.

Dibbs was insulted, then thought better of it and gave me another of his bosomy slaps on the shoulder. 'Great guy,' he said. 'I knew you were a great guy. One of the gang.' Grinning, he tucked my two bucks inside his fat wallet, and strode off to make his call.

Ah, frail, Caithleeene, but a champion of love as we set off across endless dunes.

Up a lazy river, Caithleeene . . . .

Rocky Mountain Fever, Caithleeene.

Rock of Ages, Caithleeene.

My erstwhile wife Rebecca June, driven into fits on account of my drivel and my habit of bending precious silverware and my eternal bad moods and my insistence on calling her *my frail Caithleeene.*

'Munchie's going!' someone shouted from across the room, and I looked up and there through air more shaded than the ocean floor was Saskatoon waving both arms, now pulling Munchie in front of me, shouting, 'Munchie, say goodby, Munchie, to the nice man!'

Munchie put her hands under her breasts and lifted them and blew me a kiss: 'Goodby, nice man!'

And I was moved, I was genuinely moved. I wept, and for the promise, even the promise, of a second kiss I would have followed her even *past* Saskatoon.

So much for your hand in mine, Caithleeene.

Dibbs came back. 'No answer,' he said.

'Ten o'clock, 12 o'clock rock,' I told him. 'Blue Moon, Standing on the Street Corner, Mercy-mercy, Mr. Percy.'

'Guess she's out visiting her mother.'

'Swing low,' I said. 'Looking over Jordan.'

He spilled the coins back into my pocket. Slumped his shoulders. Ah yes, old Dibbs was subdued.

'Takes all the joy out,' he said. 'You never know *what* those bitches will do! Oh well. I'm turning in.'

I took the door with him.

On the street, breathing fresh air, he shrugged and I shrugged, and each turned and headed off our separate ways.

Ah, frail your hand in mine, Caithleeene. Yours and Dibbs'. Sisters and brothers on the lam.

Shh-boom, shhh-boom . . . old buttermilk sky . . . Boo-boo-ba-boo of the night . . . .

> *I got no money*
> *and I got no friend,*
> *Me by my lonely*
> *and nearing the end.*
> *I got no wife*
> *and I got no love,*
> *Me by my lonely*
> *Living push and shove. . . .*

Two old ladies, arm-in-arm and peck-pecking their canes, looking straight ahead, were approaching me on the sidewalk.

Black glasses.

Blind.

I steered over, hugged back against a street-front door. Held my breath.

'Good evening, young man,' the two together said.

They passed on.

Ah, frail, Caithleeen. Frail. But still here. Still mine.

Gin and Tonic

THE WOMAN — THE ONE who stands here at her apartment windows in her blue stockings and blue shoes and a blue rain coat that hangs to her heels — the woman up here behind her windows high over the city's wayward slopes (Oh snow, oh hoary winter's drool!) and over the murky green waters (Needs stirring, I'll say) of Fisherman's Bay . . . is thinking: *'What next? What to do with myself today that can be half the fun yesterday was?'*

'Life *calls*!' she suddenly trumpets, surprised herself by the sound of her voice and by all the joy that, like a grinning lunatic, has leapt inside her. (I'm happy as a tick, one might conclude I've been drinkin'.)

She carefully puts down her glass.

'Eleven A.M.,' she gloats, 'all's well.'

She steps out on her narrow balcony, shivering (Merciless winter, oh sweetjesus will spring never come?), bending low and dangerously over the railing to peer inside the recessed sliding doors of the apartment below.

Feet, feet, she thinks, that's all I've ever seen. Shine your shoes, Mister-Man-Down-There.

No feet today, however. The glass needs cleaning and he ought to throw out those two dying ferns.

'I'll call Estelle,' she says. 'My good friend Estelle.'

Do *do* call Estelle, give the little lady a fine thrill.

But Estelle, it turns out (Dear me, I've split my britches), is not home. (Not in? At this hour? What *is* that elfin horror trying to prove?)

So Rebecca — woman by the window — goes back to the window and again looks out over the close-rippling water (Ten years in this place and I've yet to see a fisherman there, only boats and more boats, teensy Putt-Putts, you'd think civilized people would have better things to do) — looks out over the city slopes to the high, snowy mountains beyond (Oh fold upon fold upon fold, tedious and exhausting, but rather exquisite; yes, I *do* like it, this is such a friendly part of the world).

Oh, she thinks, what *can* I have been thinking of!

Of course.

She goes into her bedroom and takes her time selecting a nice scarf from her dresser drawer, something in a fetching complimentary blue —

'Yes, this one I think.'

and ties the silk loosely about her throat.

'Now I'm so pretty,' she remarks aloud, 'I am pretty enough to *sing sing sing!* And why not, while I'm at it, telephone Estelle?'

Estelle's phone — can you believe it? — rings and rings.

But Rebecca — following a crow's black flight across the bay (Oh look at him swerve and dive, if only I could fly like that!) — is not fooled. Oh, she's *home*, she thinks. Certainly she's home. Where else could she be but at home!

In one of her moods, possibly.

Mustn't discount her elfish moods.

One of her I-don't-want-to-see-anyone days. Doubtlessly nursing old grudges by the ton. Got the brush-off from Arnold, could be. Oh, the poor little downtrodden bird.

'None of your business,' Rebecca tells herself. 'Honey, you stay out of this.'

She laughs. Estelle is so funny when she's in her moods. No, one can't help laughing.

A fruit-cake, that's what Estelle is on her rainy-day days.

'No way out of it,' Rebecca says. 'I'd better shoot right over.'

A SWARM OF GNATS — fruit-flies, she supposes (Genus *Drosophila*, Diptera, transparent of mind and wing, oh go away, gnats!) — hangs in the air just short of Estelle's door, which Rebecca steers straight through, thinking surely they will scatter. But they come right along with her, a net of floating black dots. They swirl about, an inch up, an inch down, untouched, as she swats. 'Shoo, shoo!' she says, 'oh, scat!' Finally she wades through, knocks on Estelle's bright red door.

All the curtains drawn, house sealed up tight. Estelle, honey, is it as bad as all that?

'Yoo-hoo! It's me!'

She can hear music playing over the stereo — or radio — something classical. Harpsichordish, maybe. Old Worldish anyway.

Estelle being *grand*.

Grim *church* music to aid and abet the foul downspin.

'Let me in *at once*, darling!'

The door opens an inch and no more. The chain remains in place.

'Why have you kept me waiting here for so long?' Rebecca says. 'You should do something about this plague of wild gnats.'

All she can see of her friend Estelle is one eye in the crack. She appears to have a bandage of some sort half-covering it.

'*Go away*,' whispers Estelle.

'But I've walked miles,' replies Rebecca, not worried in the least by such rudeness. Ooo-la-la, that's Estelle. 'My feet hurt. It isn't easy in these high heels. I've probably got a blister, if you want to know. Anyway, I've got to talk to you. It's imperative. You *are* my best friend.'

The door quietly closes.

Uncanny. Oh Estelle, why are you treating me this way?

She can hear Estelle's footsteps across the floor, something clattering down (Temper, temper, oh what a temper she has!) — then the music coming on again, bit louder this time, some kind of silly piano piece, like four birds chirping from a high fence.

REBECCA SWATTED at the gnats. 'Shoo!' she said. 'Shoo! Oh,

rats! . . .' She walked slowly out to the street, her head down. At the curb she turned and regarded Estelle's house most pensively (Drab, Estelle, very drab. Most shoddy). The house was indeed drab, small and low-slung, like a Cracker Jack box down on its side, and ridiculous with its red door.

Rebecca patted one foot against the pavement. She knotted the scarf tighter against her throat.

Poor Estelle, she thought, how *can* I cheer her up?

She wondered if any of the other people in their houses along the street were watching her. I certainly should be, she thought. I would *continue the investigation* until I knew precisely what was going on. Who *is* that woman? I'd ask myself. What can she *possibly* want? Or, if I were another woman watching me, I'd think: where could she have *found* that beautiful blue coat!

I'd smoke, that's what I'd do. I'd light up a lovely blue cigarette, oh I'd have a killing-good taste of the weed.

I will anyway.

No, no, children might be watching.

An old man, four houses down, was out in his driveway washing his car. Rebecca studied him. Wouldn't it be pleasant, and a nice thing to do, to go and talk to him?

'. . . I was dropping in on my friend up the street,' she said, speaking from a distance of several dozen yards, 'but she does not appear to be receiving.'

The man, less old than she had presumed, was down on his knees sudsing a hubcap; he did not look up.

'Her name is E. Beverly Sims,' Rebecca went on, drawing closer. 'She lives in that flat house with the scrawny box hedge by the front porch. I'm sure you must know her well. Estelle is the very outgoing type, and she has a splendid figure. In a nice friendly neighbourhood such as this one is everyone must know everyone.'

The man, she now observed, stepping up beside him, had a pokey face and practically no hair. He was chewing on the nub of a cigar while squinting up at at her. She admired his way of sitting on his heels.

'Where I live it is not the least like that. I live in a small but very efficient apartment down by the Bay. A condominium. You wouldn't believe what it cost. I'm way up on the twelfth floor, and can see for miles. Do you know that huge ships pass my window at night? Far out, of course. But I have a large telescope mounted on a nice tripod. I am continuing my investigation of these ships. It's easily the most interesting hobby I ever had.'

'I'm washing this car,' the man grumbled.

Rebecca realized that the remark was somehow meant to put her in her place. She laughed.

'I can *see* that. It must have been extremely dirty.'

This comment clearly interested him. He rose up off his haunches, backed up a few paces, lit his cigar, and stared appreciatively at the automobile.

'It *was* filthy,' he said. 'My son had let this car go to the dogs.' He spat, very close to his feet, and backed up a bit more. 'They tell me young boys like nothing better than sharp cars to show off with the girls, but I give this car to my son and he has not yet got behind the wheel once.'

'Oh my,' said Rebecca. 'That is curious behaviour indeed.'

Soap suds all along the car side were drying in the sun. But the man seemed more interested in the hubcap. He stooped beside it, buffing up the chrome with his sleeve. 'Of course, he doesn't have his license yet. I give this car to him for his sixteenth birthday, but he has some months to go.' He peered up at Rebecca. 'Do you know Harold?'

'Your son? No, I —'

'You wouldn't like him. He is the most stuck-up boy I ever saw. Something of a sissy, too, you want to know the truth. Bet you can't guess why.'

'Hormones, I bet,' said Rebecca. 'I bet his hormones got sent straight up a tree.'

'Not hormones,' he said. 'His mother. His mother has pampered the little rat since the day he was born.' He paused, flipping his cigar in the dirt. Then he walked over and ground at it with his heel. 'He is out now at Symphony

School. Harold. He plays the oboe.' He picked up the cigar, examining its mangled leaves between his fingers. 'This cigar,' he said, 'it's real Havana. I got a pal sends them to me from Canada. Real cold up there. I got maybe twenty, twenty-five these rascals left.' He spread the tobacco out in his palm and poked at it with a finger. 'Real beauties, these cigars. I bet they cost my buddy a mint. But he owes me. He owes me a fortune, tell you the truth. You know why?'

Rebecca batted her eyes. 'Why?' she asked. It had struck her that this man was somewhat *odd*.

'Because I stole his wife. I stole her right out from under his nose. One day there he was, married to the prettiest woman you ever saw, and the next day she wasn't there anymore. She liked me best, you see. I had the real goods but Ralph — old Ralph — well, old Ralph didn't have *nothing* and the next thing he knew he was out in the cold. Yep, between the two of us we really put it to him.'

Rebecca considered this. She wasn't sure she liked it.

'Happy?' the man said. 'You never saw two people so happy as the wife and me. Regular love-birds.' He shot a hasty look at Rebecca. 'Then we had Harold. Beginning of the end.'

Rebecca laughed. That phrase had always been one of her favourites.

'You probably know what I mean,' he said. 'Kids! Look at Job. He had a house full of kids, but what good did they ever do him? Only more misery.'

Rebecca felt that she had been silent far too long. She thought it only right that she should point out *there was another side.*

'You would not think that,' she told him lightly, 'if you were in India, or in Greece, or even in Japan. Suppose you were in China and believed as you do? At the minimum, you'd be ostracized, and probably you'd be shot.'

'Fine by me,' he replied. 'If I had to live in those places I'd *want* to be shot.'

Rebecca walked over to the concrete steps leading up to

the front door, and sat down, crossing her legs prettily. She lit up a cigarette with her gold lighter and closed her eyes, holding her head back, blowing out the first draw of smoke in a long, measured stream.

'Nobody told you to sit there,' the man reproached her. 'This is private property.' He seemed suddenly very angry. '. . . But sit there if you want to. What the hell, whoever listens to me?'

'I'm sure you've a very strong character,' said Rebecca. 'I'm sure you must dominate any circle you enter.'

He puzzled over this a moment, then, shrugging, dropped down on his ankles again and began scrubbing the rear hubcap, his back to Rebecca. She noticed for the first time the baseball cap stuffed into his pocket. She found this intriguing, a strongly personal touch. She wondered what kind of hat he would have stuffed there had he been born in India. She found it charming, where men put their hats. He looked so round and full, stooped like that, a complete little world, total to the point even of where he put his hat. She smiled. She liked the way he bobbed up and down on his ankles, how his heels lifted up out of his shoes; his little grunts, too, were very charming. She could see an expanse of pink skin and how his underpants — swatch of black polka dots — rode up over his hips. She wondered if he would be interested in hearing what she had read about Babe Ruth — not so long ago that she had forgotten — in *The New Columbia Encyclopedia*. Sixty homers, imagine that. And born of people so rag-tail poor he had to be sent away to a training school, made to sweep floors for his daily bread. A pitcher, too. Eighty-seven wins in five years, now that was true pitching, that was real horseshoes.

She became aware after a while that the man was watching her out of the corners of his eyes.

She took off one shoe and held it above her head, shaking it, as if to dislodge pebbles. But secretly she watched him.

He dropped his sponge into the sudsy bucket, spinning on his heels. His jacket was wet up to the elbows. 'Harold's brother now,' he announced sullenly, 'he's another case. Been begging me for a car for years, but I wouldn't give him the time of day, not even if he got down on bended knee.'

Rebecca nodded. 'He must have done something extremely reprehensible,' she said.

The man gave her a blank look, then shook his head. 'Not *my* son,' he explained darkly. 'No, Norman's the *wife's* son. I keep telling him he ought to go off and live with his *real* father, but he just whines *'Aw, Dad.'* Can't even wipe his nose.' He picked up his bucket and went around to suds up the grill.

'Estelle is like that, too,' Rebecca said.

The man hiked up his pants. He looked off at the closed windows of his house and over at a stunted, leafless tree at the edge of his yard. 'That friend of yours,' he said gruffly, '. . . that Estelle, she's moved out, you know. That place is *empty* now. No, you'll waste your time knocking on *that* door.'

Rebecca decided to let this pass, and the man dropped back down to his bucket. 'I wouldn't give ten cents,' he grumbled, 'to know anybody on this block. Including your long-gone friend.'

Rebecca ignored all this. 'Beverly was her maiden name,' she told him. 'She married a man named Sims when she was twenty-eight, and although that union lasted only a short time she and Mr. Sims remain good friends to this day.' She smiled mischievously. 'Nowadays Estelle has other interests, I understand. She's in love.'

'Spit,' he said.

'Actually, she's feverish about this particular gentleman, but I have reason to believe the relationship is undergoing its difficult moments.'

'Pa-tooey,' the man said.

'I'm sure you must have seen him. He drives an orange Toyota.'

At this the man perked up. He wheeled about, pointing to a spot on the street vaguely in front of Estelle's house. 'Orange?' he said. Rebecca took this to mean that he had seen the car in question parked out in front of Estelle's house through nights too numerous to mention.

'They may be good cars,' he said gruffly, 'but only a traitor would buy one.' He smacked a flat, wet hand against the top of his own automobile. 'I've seen him,' he said. 'He wears a hat.'

This news tantalized Rebecca. She had never seen Estelle's lover wearing a chapeau of any sort. She stood up now. She had smoked her cigarette and had her visit and was now ready to leave.

'Where you going?' the man asked her.

She smiled, surprised. 'Why, I don't know,' she said. 'I haven't thought about it.'

He strode past her to the side of the house, beckoning. 'Come inside,' he grumbled. 'Something to show you. I bought my son a .22 for his birthday. I've got it on a gun rack in the den. I don't suppose you shoot, being a woman — my wife *hates* it — but what I say is if Harold doesn't go out and shoot something with it the very minute he turns sixteen I'm going to throw him out of the house.' He shoved his hands deep into his jacket pockets, scowling back at Rebecca who was lingering. 'It beats me,' he said, 'why women don't like hunting. And fishing. There is not anything more fun than that. Character-building, too. My old man had me out on the marsh with a rifle in my arms before I was two years old. Women! I'll tell you about women. Women have got themselves into this trouble out of their own choosing. They deserve everything they get. Bunch of fools, if you ask me. Silliest thing on two feet. Look at you, for instance. All sky-baby-blue in that silly rain coat and those silly shoes. Well, it's *feminine* all right, but that's all I can say for it.'

Rebecca laughed, a low breasty chuckle that brightened her face. She loved insults. She wished he'd say something else — perhaps about her hair or her nice scarf or her blue pocket-book.

She wished he'd put on his funny little cap.

139

'Come on,' he ordered. 'Want to show you that gun.'

Rebecca was tempted. Few things pleased her more than seeing how other people lived. She could imagine herself inside browsing through his cupboards, checking out cereal boxes, opening the refrigerator door to read out the brand names on frozen foods. But she'd been looking at Estelle's house; she was certain she'd seen the front curtain move. 'No thank you,' she said. 'Perhaps another time. I'm often in the neighbourhood.'

'Buzz off then,' he said. 'Who asked you? I got better things to do.'

THE GNATS HAD MOVED on from Estelle's door. They were now up around the telephone wire where it entered the house, a larger body now, black patch silently lifting and falling, swaying, against the clear blue sky.

'It's me again,' Rebecca called, knocking.

The house was silent. Four or five rolled newspapers were on the ground beneath the hedge, soiled and wet, further indication to Rebecca that Estelle's love life had reached the cutthroat stage.

'I've brought you your reading matter!' she shouted, bent at the keyhole, thinking she detected shadowy movement inside.

'I'll huff and I'll puff!' she called. 'Stand back!'

Estelle didn't respond.

A tomb.

THE BACK OF THE HOUSE was deserted, too. Curtains were drawn over the windows, and a beautiful spider web had been spun over the upper portion of the door. Crumpled newspaper filled a hole down in the corner of one cracked window. Under the roof line stretched a series of old hornets' nests, or dirt-daubers' sturdy quarters. The garbage can was overturned, but empty. A rusty barbecue stand was down on its side in the tall grass. Numerous tin cans and milk cartons littered the area; a huge cardboard lay flattened by the rain.

Rebecca took her time contemplating the debris, seated in a white metal chair out near where a composting fixture once had stood. She smoked, and pitched her head back to catch the sunshine. She would have been happy, if only she had a drink to sip on.

Gloves, she thought. Why haven't I bought myself a pair of nice blue gloves?

The silence of the place fascinated her. She realized she was genuinely enjoying this.

A large fluffy cat, golden in colour, hopped up on the picnic table in the neighbouring yard. It took turns idly scrutinizing her, and, just as idly, licking its fur.

'Gin,' said Rebecca. 'Gin and tonic, I think.'

And she stayed on another ten minutes or so, enjoying the invisible drink.

Someone not far away was calling. A woman's fragile, unhurried voice repeating: '*Oro!* ... *Oro!* ... *Come home, Oro.*'

Very musical, Rebecca thought.

A breeze played gently across her face, further subduing her mood, and she let herself drift along in a sweet, dreamy doze, seeing the world before her as though through a haze in which all things moved in tranquil, harmonic order, pleasant and kind.

The sun dropped down rays thick as a lattice fence, golden and alluring.

What splendour, she thought. I could be in someone's enchanted garden.

AFTERWARDS, drawing the blue collar up against her neck, feeling somewhat chilled, she stepped again up to Estelle's rear window. She rapped on the glass, looking for a peephole through the curtains.

'Estelle? Estelle, darling, please open the door.'

She heard a quick catch of breath, within, and could feel Estelle's presence on the other side of the wall.

'It's lovely out here, it truly is. You should come out and

talk to me. He hasn't hurt you, has he?' She heard a whisper of footsteps, the creak of floor-boards, and beat her knuckles sharply against the window. 'Oh don't be unhappy!' she pleaded. 'Please let me in. He isn't worth this pining, Estelle. . . .'

The floor creaked again.

A cat squawled somewhere in the neighbourhood, much as if someone were repeatedly pulling its tail.

Rebecca stiffened; she shivered. She whipped her head around, certain that someone had stolen up and was about to hit her on the head.

No. . . .

A very old man, with an enormous stomach, wearing a checkered shirt and carrying his shoes in his hands, was out on the steps next door, watching her. He leaned against the door-frame, putting on one shoe. Then he leaned the opposite way and put on the other.

'I think she's left that place,' he said. 'I think she moved out four, five days ago.'

Rebecca smiled at him.

The man backed up, slowly withdrawing into the house.

Nearby, someone was singing, or perhaps it was a radio.

Rebecca stared a moment at the dusty, faded newspaper stuffed into the window crack. 'I've got my troubles too, Estelle,' she said. 'My phone rings every night. It's that man I told you about. He refuses to let up. Every night I think "well, tonight he's going to threaten me" . . . but he never quite does. He's extremely cunning. What do I do, Estelle?'

When Estelle didn't answer, Rebecca went up on tiptoe and tugged the stiff paper free. Then she went up again on tiptoe, straightened her arm, and poked her hand into the small opening. She worked her hand past the jagged glass and past the curtain edge and thrust her arm deeper into the room. It felt cold, very cold, in there.

Something brushed or cut or struck against her flesh and with a faint cry of pain, of fear, she snatched back her arm.

Shards of glass tinkled down, her heel twisted in the uneven dirt and she stumbled back, holding in her breath; she staggered, banged one knee against dirt, then lost her balance totally and landed gracelessly on one hip.

Dizzily, she got to her feet. Her coat sleeve was torn, scar in the blue fabric scarcely larger than a dime; a straight line of blood was popping up in droplets across the backside of her hand. It stung.

'You've cut me, Estelle,' she said, her voice calm, amazed.

She had a clear vision of Estelle inside the cold room, pressed against the wall, eyes slitted, knife poised, waiting for her again to poke through her arm.

But she wasn't sure. It could have been the glass.

She licked the line clean, hastily pulled free her scarf, and wrapped it around her hand.

'That was uncalled-for, Estelle. That was very mean.'

She drew back, watching the window.

'But I forgive you.'

At the corner of the house she turned, calling again.

'I know you're not yourself today. I really wish you'd let me help you.'

SHE WENT ONCE MORE to the front of the house and sat down on Estelle's stoop, brooding on this turn of events.

No, the fault wasn't Estelle's. The fault was Arnold's.

She unfolded one of the newspapers. The moisture had soaked through and the sheet had to be peeled apart. Displayed across the front page was a photograph of Nureyev leaping, his legs flung wide, bare buttocks to the camera, arrow pointing to where his tights had ripped. DANCER SHOWS TRUE FORM, the caption read. But Rebecca shivered at the black headlines. Shivered, and let her head swoop down against the page. 58 DIE IN BLOOD-BATH . . . OIL RIG GOES DOWN OFF NEWFOUNDLAND, NO SURVIVORS . . . WARSAW ERUPTS.

Yes, she thought, and my mother is dead, my husband has

left me, I have no children, hardly any life, and no one knows anything at all — or cares! — about poor Rebecca.

But when her head came up she was ruefully smiling.

Yes, all true, she thought, but we shall continue the investigation.

She turned, peering through Estelle's keyhole.

'Peace Promised for One Zillion Years!' she shouted. 'Happiness Lays Golden Egg! . . . Man Steps in Pot-hole, Breaks Leg!'

She removed the scarf from her hand and closely observed the wound. 'Nineteen Stitches Required!' she called. 'Noted Plastic Surgeon Called In! . . . Lady Recovers from Heartless Attack!'

The tear in the coat bothered her more. She wondered whether a good seamstress could save the day.

A boy was approaching, yet some distance down the street, slouching, his hands deep into his pockets, small black case tucked up under one arm, his face white as plaster in the sunlight.

Harold.

The man who had been washing the car was no longer in the yard, nor was the car. A woman now stood out in front of the house, arms crossed over her chest. She was looking past Rebecca at the dawdling boy. She wore a print dress, too bold for her thick figure; the hem hung unevenly and the grass cut off her legs. She called wanly to the boy:

'Harold! Harold! He hit me, Harold!'

Harold stopped. Now nearly abreast of Estelle's house, he looked not at his mother but at Rebecca cooly watching from the stoop.

'You don't live there,' he said to her. 'That place is deserted.'

Rebecca loved this frontal approach. He was sullen, nasty even, but she wanted to reach out and hug him. He was abusive, yes, but it seemed to her that those who were most insulting were also those who most willingly offered enthusiastic praise.

'What's that under your arm?' she asked him. 'Is that an oboe?'

The boy's face clouded. He kicked a shoe against the pavement, standing with his body bent like a quarter moon.

'I wish you'd play for me,' Rebecca said. 'I haven't heard an oboist play really well in years.'

'Who are you?' he growled. 'What are you doing in our neighbourhood?'

'*Harold! He hit me, Harold,*' called his mother.

The boy put his case on the sidewalk and, crouching, took the instrument from it, polishing the bulbous end on his sleeve.

'I give the pitch to the whole orchestra,' he said, standing, glaring at Rebecca.

He blew a strong, high note, which then seemed to falter — but the note came back stronger, more penetrating, thin, only a little plaintive, and it intensified and kept on coming.

'*Harold!*' called the mother. '*He really hit me hard.*'

His mother now stood at the edge of her yard, her hands twisting around the narrow trunk of a leafless tree.

The boy scowled at Rebecca. 'Sure, I could play,' he said. 'But I won't. Harold only plays for money.'

Rebecca nodded doubtfully, her thoughts drifting, watching the swarm of gnats at the side of the house, hovering a few feet above the scraggly grass.

'You're a very good-looking boy,' Rebecca said. 'I'll bet you must be every inch of six feet tall.'

'*He hurt me, Harold!*'

The boy came up and sat down on the stoop beside Rebecca.

'I'm very advanced for my age,' he told her. 'I'm very unusual. In fact, I'm eccentric.'

'Well, it is a strange neighbourhood,' she said.

'Not that strange. The woman who lived here — what was her name?'

'Estelle.'

'Estelle was strange. I saw her one night out back of this

house, practically naked — in a flowing gown, I mean — down on her knees in front of that chair she's got back there, bowing and bowing, like an Arab. *That's* strange.'

Rebecca smiled. 'Not if you know Estelle,' she replied softly.

Across the way his mother advanced a few paces, her footsteps weighted, as if deep holes were opening in front of her. When she saw them looking at her she backed up, returning hastily to the tree.

The boy moistened the mouthpiece, allowed his head to settle deep between his shoulders, then played several quick, rather piercing, notes. 'Listen to this,' he said.

He closed his eyes.

He played.

When the last lingering note faded, Rebecca, only now opening her eyes, clapped enthusiastically. 'Oh God,' she sighed, genuinely moved: 'You're going to be immortal.'

The boy stretched out one hand, palm upwards.

'I'm bleeding, Harold!' his mother called.

Rebecca opened her purse. She looked thoughtfully at her bills, then unsnapped her change purse, and dropped two quarters into his hand.

The boy stared glumly at the coins. 'What can this buy?' he asked.

'Happiness,' Rebecca said. And she smiled in a bewitched way, as if indeed it had.

The boy walked away, pointing with his instrument to the swarm of gnats.

'Those gnats are mating,' he said.

At his yard he turned and went on past his mother without a word and entered the house and a few seconds later she left the tree and scooted in after him.

Rebecca leaned back against Estelle's door. 'The music was lovely, wasn't it?' she said. 'I wonder where such genius comes from.'

It seemed to her that from inside the house there came a whispery, half-strangled *yes!*

Rebecca stayed on, pursuing stray thoughts as they popped into her head. Harold's music, unquestionably very beautiful, had put the Garden of Eden into her mind. A kind of dreamy, springtime garden. Yet now several hundred men, no larger than bees, were erecting a barbed-wire fence around the place.

She laughed. How silly.

'A blight has hit the garden,' she said.

Men with rifles were up sniping from their towers. *Plunk plunk plunk!* Bullets stirred up soft puffs of dust in the arid soil.

Off in the corner, darkened, the Tree of Knowledge hunkered down, like a rat gone fat from too much wine and cheese. The bullets went on plunking.

Plunk plunk plunk!

Rebecca giggled. It's absurd, she thought, but what can be done about it?

'*Aim over their heads,*' a voice said. '*We don't want to harm anyone.*'

Rebecca's heart caught. She recognized that voice.

'*Well, one or two,*' God said, '*as an example.*'

Two or three hundred of the small bee people began to fall. They rolled down into the grass, kicked and lay still, or they screamed and went limp, snagged on the wire.

Plunk plunk plunk!

Rebecca leaped up, throwing her hands over her eyes. 'Estelle,' she said, 'I've just had the most awful vision!' She knocked again on Estelle's door, and kicked at it, and put her eye against the keyhole, and for a moment believed she saw another eye looking back — but then decided this was nonsense, since Estelle lacked any such curiosity. No, Estelle, after such a busy day, would be spread out on her bed, damp cloth across her brow, claiming headaches, claiming troubles, agony too painful to mention.

I too was once like that, Rebecca thought. I believed I didn't have a friend in the world.

Like something shoved over the edge . . . and still falling.

But she had learned better long ago. People valued her. Friends were ever eager to see her. They let her know without any guile or trickery — without any reservations whatsoever — that their doors were always open.

'Anytime, Rebecca. For you we are always home.'

She brushed off the seat of her rain coat, fluffed her hair, and started towards the street. 'I'm going now!' she called. '. . . Take care of yourself! . . . Enjoyed visiting! . . . See you tomorrow!'

Maybe. Maybe she would see her tomorrow.

At any moment she expected to see Estelle yanking open the door, flinging herself down the path, embracing and pulling her back.

'Chin up, darling! . . . Accept no wooden nickels!'

But the red door remained firmly shut.

She wondered what Harold would be doing. Where Arnold would be in his orange Toyota.

What next? Who to see?

She'd go home first, laze around a bit. Have a quiet smoke, perhaps a nice gin and tonic. Watch the big, distant ships hulking ever so silently by on Fisherman's Bay. Watch the fog — watch darkness — descend slowly over the water.

Think this matter through.

Think about tomorrow.